COME, LLAMAS

§ 1

COME, LLAMAS

JENNIFER MORRIS

Delacorte Press

Published by
Delacorte Press
an imprint of
Random House Children's Books
a division of Random House, Inc.
New York

Visit us on the Web! www.randomhouse.com/kids
Educators and librarians, for a variety of teaching tools, visit us at
www.randomhouse.com/teachers

Library of Congress Cataloging-in-Publication Data

Morris, Jennifer.
    Come llamas / Jennifer Morris.
       p. cm.
    Summary: Nine-year-old J. T. Kinnaman is given his first llama to raise on his
family's Alaskan ranch.
    ISBN 0-385-73197-3 (trade) — ISBN 0-385-90229-8 (glb)
    [1. Llama farms—Fiction. 2. Ranch life—Alaska—Fiction. 3. Llamas—Fiction.
4. Grandfathers—Fiction. 5. Alaska—Fiction.] I. Title.
    PZ7.M82823Co 2005
    [Fic]—dc22   2004000900

The text of this book is set in 12-point Baskerville BE Regular.

Book design by Angela Carlino

Printed in the United States of America

February 2005

10 9 8 7 6 5 4 3 2 1

BVG

For Brady, Eli, and Zoë, and in fond memory of my grandfather, Howard Kenneth Hoyt, who lived a life of hope and adventure

Soli Deo Gloria!

1

I opened the barn door and took a deep breath. The scent of straw and sweet timothy hay filled the night air. All around me, our llamas hummed and chewed. It sounded like *grum, grum.* My grandad called it their "wild music."

Shining my flashlight, I walked down the long aisle, checking each stall for babies. Any day now, these pregnant llamas would drop their crias. Grandad had made a deal with me the past summer and I hadn't forgotten it: the first cria born this spring was mine, the start of my herd. I would finally have my very own llama to raise.

JT Kinnaman, llama rancher.

Grandad said nine was old enough to start making my contribution to Kinnaman Ranch. My brother, Greg, and my dad and Uncle Del all got their first llamas when they were my age. I wanted to raise a champion show llama, or maybe a brave guard, a cart puller, or a strong packer. I knew I would be an awesome llama farmer. I'd bet my favorite baseball on that.

All spring, I had been praying that my cria would be out of our smartest llama, Snow. She was the ranch's trainer llama, the one Grandad used to teach new owners before they took their llamas home. I learned on her, too. I learned to pack her for hiking trips and how to give her orders like *cush* and *stand*. She would lie down and stand up for me, even though most of the other llamas wouldn't. She was also the most beautiful llama on Kinnaman Ranch—pure white with a long, straight neck.

I tiptoed along, shining my light back and forth. Snow's stall was the last one in the row. I'd ridden her since I was three, and thought of her as mine. There is nothing like a strong soft llama carrying you up a mountain, I can promise that. But I hadn't ridden her that winter, of course, because of the growing cria. Whenever I brought her fresh hay or filled her water bucket, I told her I would take good care of her baby.

This spring would be the best year yet for crias on Kinnaman Ranch, Grandad said. The snow was starting to melt, and runoff was filling the creeks around our farm. Soon the water would be high and our fields would be covered with green grass and prancing, running crias.

"Hey, girl," I called softly. I shined the light into Snow's stall. All llamas, and especially grouchy pregnant llamas, dislike a surprise. "Hey." Usually she swung her face over the gate to greet me with a whiffle—a puff of air—and take an alfalfa biscuit from my hand. When she didn't come to the stall door, I peered over the wall.

She lay on her side, panting. I unlatched the door and stepped in. "Snow?" Her brown eyes rolled toward me. Llamas tuck their legs under them when they sleep; they don't lie flat unless they're sick or hurt.

Or having trouble birthing a cria.

I checked under her tail. There was one tiny black hoof.

I ran out of the barn, across the yard, and up the steps, bursting through the mudroom and into the kitchen. "Dad!"

Dad and Grandad looked up from the table.

"Snow's down! And her cria's coming!"

Dad got up, hurrying past me to the mudroom. Grandad followed, putting his cap on and shoving his feet into his boots. "Where's Greg?"

"Changing the starter on the crummy," I said. Our old pickup truck always needed work.

"Then we'll need your help, JT. Wash your hands and get the medicine bag," Grandad said.

I scrubbed my hands, ran to the shop, grabbed the bag, and sprinted through the night air back to Snow's stall.

Dad and Grandad knelt next to her, their backs hunched at the same angle, wearing matching blue Kinnaman Ranch caps. Dad put gloves on and said, "Squirt iodine on my hands, Joey." I dug the bottle out of the bag and squirted the brown liquid on his gloves. Grandad laid tools on a blanket—a scalpel, cutters, a clamp, and twine. "JT, you be ready to hand these to your dad when he needs them."

My heart was pounding so hard, I could feel it through my shirt. I said the names of the tools over and over to myself. Grandad gently lay across Snow's neck to hold her down, then said, "Ready."

Snow grunted and Dad pulled. "Rope, Joe."

Rope?

I fumbled for the twine and handed it to him. Dad tied it around the cria's ankles, then sat back on his heels and waited. Snow thrashed around, then grunted, and Dad reached in and pulled. "Come on, little llama," he coaxed. He grimaced, his forehead turning red. Grandad stroked Snow's white cheek and her neck, telling her it would be all right.

Dad stopped pulling and rubbed his arm over his face. "Must be big. Who's the sire?"

"Tumtum," Grandad said.

Dad whistled. He rested one hand on Snow's leg.

"Hang in there, girl," he said. Tumtum was Greg's llama, and the largest llama on Kinnaman Ranch, probably in all of Alaska—more than four hundred pounds.

Grandad petted Snow and told her it would be over soon. The warm cozy barn was starting to feel hot and sticky. Bits of hay stuck to the sweat on my forehead.

Snow's eyes rolled and she grunted again. Dad braced himself and pulled. The head came out, and then a slimy gray cria slid onto the straw. I turned away.

Grandad sat on his heels and Snow's ears swiveled toward the cria. She wanted to sniff the baby, but she was too tired. She laid her head down. Grandad said, "JT, take a look at that."

I looked back at the tiny wet llama. It was amazing and gross at the same time. "Wow." Then I looked at Snow, stretched out flat like roadkill. "Is she okay?"

"She'll be all right," Grandad said, rubbing the cria with a towel. "But he's kind of small. Doesn't look like much for all this trouble. Maybe twelve pounds. Come on, baby, breathe."

Dad was feeling around Snow's belly. He held his palm against her side. "Well, I'll be," he said.

"What?"

"We've got another heartbeat. Snow here is having twins."

"Twins!" I said. Llamas hardly ever have twins.

"No time to lose. Her contractions will start up again soon. Is he breathing?"

Grandad cut the cord with the scalpel, then suctioned the cria's nose. "Not yet. But there's still hope." He rubbed the cria's chest, pushing on his ribs.

I bent over the little face. He was gray like morning fog. The cria's eyes were closed. I wiped his leathery nostrils and little lips. "Breathe, little guy."

Grandad hung the cria upside down to get fluid out of his airway. Nothing. He worked on it awhile longer, then set the body down and sighed. "That's a shame," he said.

I stood staring at it. It looked so perfect, a perfect little llama. "What's the matter?"

"We might never know. We lost that one." Grandad put his arm around me.

That was supposed to be my llama.

"Rope," Dad said, startling me.

I gave him the rope and he tied it around another little black hoof. Suddenly Snow stood. Her belly contracted and another cria slid out headfirst, landing on the straw with a thump.

This cria was black as night, with a tiny white star between his ears. "He's not breathing either," Dad said.

Grandad knelt over the body, sucking mucus out of its nostrils with a nasal syringe. "Come on," he whispered.

Dad thumped it on the chest a couple of times, then stood and hung it upside down. "It's tiny."

"We're not losing them both." Grandad leaned over and blew a short puff in the cria's face.

Suddenly the cria sneezed and started breathing. "That's better," Grandad said. "JT, wipe out his nose and mouth so he can breathe easier, then dry him off."

I knelt down and took a look at the newest Kinnaman llama. I dried his mouth and nose and rubbed him with the towel.

Following Grandad's instructions, I cut the umbilical cord, untied the rope, and stretched each leg out to check for broken bones. I looked in his ears. Last, I checked to be sure the cord had quit bleeding. It was wrinkled like a deflated balloon. The cria's black eyes were clear and bright—like they were made of oil. He blinked at me.

"Three minutes," Grandad warned. "I'll get rid of this carcass before she smells it and gets upset." He picked up the gray cria and stepped out of the stall.

"Three minutes until what?" I asked.

"You can't handle a newborn cria longer than three minutes, or else he'll think he's your baby and not Snow's. Then he'll starve," Dad said. He gave Snow a shot and rubbed her hip muscle where it went in. "Now come on. We've got to get out of here."

Snow stepped gingerly to the water bucket for a long drink. Then she stood over the black cria, telling me with her big brown eyes to go away.

Dad stepped outside the stall and looked back.

"We'll see how he does," Dad said. "He sure is a little guy, isn't he?"

"I'll say," said Grandad. He tipped back his cap and scratched at his bald spot. "See that star, JT?" He pointed at the white spot on the cria's head. "That means he'll bring good luck to his owner."

"Hey, Pop, let me carry that," Dad said. "You're supposed to take it easy, remember?"

"I'm fine, Robert."

"Just let me carry it, Pop." Dad took the dead cria by the back hooves.

I waited, holding my breath, hoping Grandad would say it. We leaned over the stall and watched Snow sniff the cria from head to toe. When I couldn't stand it another second, I said, "Grandad, do you remember last summer?"

"Last summer? I'm eighty-six, JT. I don't remember yesterday!" He winked at Dad, who winked back.

"*Grandad,*" I said. "You promised I could have the first cria of this year's batch."

Grandad picked up the blanket and bucket. "Did I, now?" He and Dad started down the aisle.

"Did you, Pop?"

"Yes, he did," I said.

"Get the light, Joey," said Dad.

I took one last look at the little black cria before snapping the light off. What if Grandad changed his mind? What if Grandad thought this one was too small or too sick for me to care for? Something in me ached to call him mine. I caught up with them outside the door.

Dad gently set the dead cria in the burn pit and started the fire.

"Why don't we bury him?" I asked.

"We have to burn a carcass," Grandad said. "Burying it would attract every meat-eater around." He looked at the tops of Little Sister and Big Sister and the range surrounding Kinnaman Ranch. "Say, Robert, we ought to check the perimeter fence for weak spots. Gabby tells me the bears are going to be hungry this year."

"How does he know, Grandad?" I asked.

"I suppose from living up on the mountain and watching them like he does. Says the trappers have been finding their catch torn right out of the traps," Grandad said. "If Gabby says the bears are going to be bad, I tend to lean on his advice."

"Well," I said, "does Gabby happen to say anything about giving me a llama?"

Grandad and Dad laughed into the night air. We dropped our supplies off at the shop, and when Grandad came out, he had another Kinnaman Ranch cap in his hand. Only Kinnaman ranchers were allowed to wear them. My brother, Greg, got his when he was nine. Uncle Del got his years ago, then gave it back to work on computers in Anchorage.

"You're responsible for him," Grandad said. "We'll

help you if you need it, but he's your responsibility. Feeding, training, worming. Everything."

"I know." I stood up straight and tall. "I can do it."

Grandad put the cap on my head and shook my hand. "Congratulations, JT. He's a fine-looking llama."

"Thanks. How much luck do you think that star is worth?"

Grandad put his hand to his mouth and leaned toward me, like he was telling a secret. "Hard work is the best luck you'll ever have, JT."

Dad laughed. "Be careful that cap doesn't fall right off."

I stood under the moon with the barns and fields of Kinnaman Ranch around me. I felt like I owned it all. One day, I would. I finally wore the blue corduroy cap just like Dad and Grandad. I had a herd to care for now, a small one, but a herd just the same. My heart swelled with pride. "It fits just fine."

"Look." Grandad pointed up at the sky. A great bald eagle soared across the valley, alighting in a tree on Big Sister Mountain. "There he is."

It was Old Timer, Grandad's favorite eagle. He'd watched Old Timer grow from an eaglet, before I was born, to a white-headed eagle with a six-foot wingspan.

"Life keeps on." Grandad smiled. "Old Timer always comes out when Kinnaman Ranch is changing." He put his hand on my shoulder. "We've got a new partner, Robert."

I grinned and hugged him. Dad smiled. "Are you sure that cap fits, son?"

"I'm sure."

Much later, after Grandad was asleep, snoring in his bed by the window, I crawled out of bed and took the cap off my bedpost. I unsnapped it and tightened it, just to be sure.

2

The next morning I was awake before the cold Alaska sun, before Dad or Greg or Mom. I thought I was up before Grandad, too. I figured I might as well get started taking care of my herd. I got dressed and tiptoed to the door. I touched the doorknob.

"Be sure to check his cord, JT."

I laughed. "Morning, Grandad." No matter how early I got up, I could never beat him. And he always seemed to know what I was thinking.

"You've got to watch him carefully for infection. He'll get a fever first, then lose his appetite and get dehydrated. I've lost a llama in a day. If the cord looks red or swollen or is oozing, or if he's hot, you've got an infection to deal with and you need help fast."

"I'll check it."

"And remember—"

"Three minutes," I said. "Got it."

"Good."

The mountains were silver with moonlight and the ground was covered with frost. The sun came slowly in the spring. There were about six hours of daylight now, but minute by minute the days got longer, and they would keep getting longer until the snow melted and the ground was dry. By June there would be no darkness at all—we'd have a Midnight Sun baseball game and a barbecue on the night of the summer solstice, June twenty-first. Spring was my favorite time of year and this was my favorite place on earth. Not that I'd been all that many places, but I didn't have to travel the world to know I'd never leave.

I took a small halter and the bottle of iodine from the shop and pulled open the barn door.

The dams rustled and hummed when they heard the door creak. I poked my head into every stall, but there weren't any more crias. At Snow's stall, I unlatched the door and slipped inside. Snow was snuggled next to the cria, her belly to his back. I gave her fresh water and a flake of hay. She sniffed the sweet smell of it and stood. "Hey," I greeted her. "Hey, Snow." I petted her ears and her neck and she whiffled my face. I gave her an alfalfa biscuit. Then the cria woke up.

He shoved his front legs out, trying to set his little hooves against the cement floor. Then he straightened his back legs, pushing until he stood. He wobbled a little, looking around like he didn't know what he'd done. I felt like clapping. "Good job," I whispered. He took a shaky step toward Snow, then nuzzled around until he found the milk. He was done after a few drinks and started exploring: sniffing the latch, the wood, the water bucket. I sat on the floor and let him sniff me. He nuzzled my ear and I laughed. "I'm JT," I told him. "Most people call me Joey, but I like JT." When I was seven, I told the family I wanted to be called JT, not Joey anymore. The only people who switched were my best friend, Nicky, and Grandad. Everyone else still calls me Joey. I wish they wouldn't. JT sounds more grown-up to me. It stands for Joseph Turre Kinnaman, the youngest Kinnaman.

I petted him. "You're the first of my herd." The cria sneezed.

I took the halter and slipped it over his muzzle, buckling it behind his ears. Kinnaman ranchers halter crias right away, so they grow up used to the way it feels. He shook his little head. I dabbed iodine on his umbilical cord, which now hung from his belly like a brown banana peel. He kicked at my hand. "Sorry, buddy. Have to," I whispered. I scratched behind his ears. Baby fiber is the softest thing on earth, softer than cotton candy from the Alaska State Fair in Palmer, which I'd been to twice. Softer than cotton balls, softer than my mom's hair. He smelled like straw and llama musk. "What will we do with you, buddy?"

Snow stomped and hummed. "Okay," I said, slipping the halter off. I stepped out of the stall and latched the door. My three minutes were up.

Up and down the aisles I went with bucket after bucket of water and flakes of hay. After I'd fed and watered the rest of the pregnant llamas, I went back to Snow's stall.

"Let's go," I said, opening the door. I led Snow out of the stall. The cria bawled, then clumsily ran to her side. I led them to the scale, then gently lifted the cria up and weighed him. Grandad was right. He *was* a little guy, half the size of most newborns.

After I put them away, I got Snow's breeding record from the shop file and wrote that she'd birthed one live and one stillborn cria, and the date.

I made a new card for the cria, too. I filled in the date, his markings, and his weight. He was little, but he would grow. Maybe he would become a brave guard llama like Sentry or Tex. Or maybe he would pack for tourists hiking through Denali like Tessa and Sammy did, or take home Best of Show at the fair like Snow did year after year. There was hope for him yet.

I looked at the line for his name. Maybe it was his

little cry, or how soft he was, but "Elmo" came to mind. I wrote it in my best handwriting, then added *Owner: JT Kinnaman.*

I hurried through the rest of my chores. When I was finished, I stopped by Snow's stall. "I named him Elmo," I told her. She lifted her head, and her fuzzy lips explored the rim of my cap. The cria was snuggled down in the warm straw, napping. For his first year, he would stay with Snow. When he turned one year old, he'd move to the yearling herd—the toddlers, Grandad called them. When he turned two, he'd move on to the bachelor herd, away from the females. The bachelor year was the big year of a cria's life—the year of his first clipping, and of proving his nature. If he was big and had thick, woolly fiber, he'd be a sire. I hoped not, though: Buck and Tumtum, the sires of Kinnaman Ranch, were rowdy and obnoxious. If he was calm and obedient, he'd be a packer. If he was bold and curious, a guard. If he was all those things plus intelligent, he could pull a cart. And no matter what he grew up to be, he still had to learn to cush, stand, and hold still for shearing.

I had all kinds of hopes for Elmo. But first he needed to grow up.

I lifted my cap and scratched my head. "Welcome to Kinnaman Ranch, Elmo," I told the little black llama.

3

In the house, my family was in motion. Mom, Dad, Grandad, and Greg were sitting at the kitchen table. I mixed a cup of hot mud: hot milk, a splash of coffee, and a lot of honey. It was the same color as Alaska's spring mud, and tasted great. I held the cup in my hand like Grandad did, thumb on the rim and fingers on the handle, sipping as Dad finished reading aloud from Proverbs. Then I grabbed a biscuit. When I took a bite and dropped crumbs on the floor, Grandad looked up: "Set a minute, son. My coffee's almost gone."

I plunked on the bench next to Greg. Mom put her hand on my head. "How are the dams?"

"Great. You should come out and see the new baby."

"I will." She smiled at me.

I swallowed my biscuit and drained my cup. "Can I go practice now?"

"Are they fed?"

"Yep."

"Fresh water?"

"Yep."

"Got your mitt?"

"Yep." I got up and ran to the mudroom. I took off my boots, put on my cleats, and opened the back door. "Grandad! Coming?"

Grandad got up from the table, taking one last swig of coffee. "Wouldn't miss it."

"Why don't you let Greg take him out this morning, Turre?" Mom asked.

Dad picked up the newspaper and started reading the sports section.

Grandad's eyebrows went up. "And miss all the fun? JT's got tryouts this afternoon."

Mom leaned toward him. "I know, but . . . you seem a little pale today."

"Probably just the light in here," Grandad said. "There's nothing to fuss about."

Mom raised her eyebrows at Dad and he shook his head. I wished they would let us go already.

Greg leaned back. "Isn't it your turn to muck out the big barn, squirt?"

"It's yours, and you know it," I said.

Greg looked at Mom. "Well," he sighed, flinging his hands up. "You can't blame a guy for trying to get out of a little work."

Everyone laughed. Grandad cackled. "Don't get lazy on us, Greg. But come out and throw the ball with us first if you want."

"I got your mitt." I held it up for Grandad to see.

He smoothed his hair sideways over his bald spot and put on his cap. "Then let's go, boys."

"Greg," Mom said in a warning voice.

"I know, Mom." Greg shoved his feet into his cleats.

"I'll get our gear," I called. I ran to the machine shed and shoved the door open, then started the FourTrax. It was the easiest way to get around Fireweed, and everyone I knew rode one.

I put it in reverse and pushed the throttle with my thumb. The FourTrax shot backward into the yard. Greg the mechanical whiz had been tinkering with the engine again. Greg was barely seventeen, but *everything* he did was great—engines, baseball, and llama ranching—and he never let me forget it. Thanks to him I drove the fastest four-wheeler in school.

Grandad started slowly across the gravel, then stopped and stood still, like he'd forgotten where he was headed.

"Are you coming, Grandad?"

"Aren't I your head pitching coach?" Grandad

tipped the bill of his cap back and smiled. He walked up and put one hand on the seat.

"Well, sure, but—"

"So I'm going. Who's driving?"

Greg ran out with his mitt and he and I shouted together, "I'll drive!"

Grandad looked at us, his blue eyes sparkling like normal. "Greg on the way out, JT on the way back."

"Can't we take both four-wheelers?" I asked, clasping my hands together.

"Dad needs the other one. He's driving the packer herd out to the north field today," said Greg.

"But that means I have to ride on the—"

"Cargo rack." Greg jerked his thumb toward the metal rack over the back tires. I climbed on and Grandad handed me the bucket of balls and mitts.

"That'll be a bumpy ride," Grandad said pleasantly, easing himself on behind Greg and positioning his feet on the pegs. "But your tail can take it better than mine. Tallyho, Greg."

The ride out to the back field was a pretty one, at least, and I was happy. I thought of Elmo. He was the best-looking llama I'd seen, even if he was a bit small.

I picked up a ball and squeezed it. Lately Mom was making Greg come out and practice with us, but I liked just Grandad and me best. Right after a baseball game last summer, I'd told Grandad a secret—I wanted to pitch for my team, the Eagles. I knew I was good enough, but Bo Brickland had been doing it since the seven-and-under league. I asked Grandad if he would help me learn.

He had nodded very seriously. He always knew when things were important to me. "You'll need to practice." He went out to the woodshed and sawed and hammered. He nailed a big square on a sawhorse about waist high. "Here's your strike zone," he said. "We'll start tonight."

After dinner, he'd rooted around in the attic until he came up with his old baseball glove. It looked like it had been run over by a tractor and left to rot, but he put it on anyway. He squeezed it a few times and said, "I think she has a few more catches in her." He punched the palm. Then he oiled it, and he oiled my glove, too.

I didn't even ask Grandad to keep our pitching practice a secret, he just did. A few months later, Greg wanted to use the strike box boards for a new fish trap and I had to explain why he couldn't take it apart. Greg didn't make fun of me at all, though, just said he'd get some other wood. And most every morning, even in the dead of winter, Grandad and I drove out to the back field to practice. Tryouts were that night after school, and I was ready.

We drove along the perimeter at the base of the mountain. The mountain looked blue-spruce colored, with a pale sky behind it. No sign of the sun yet, but there wasn't much in March anyway. It would come later.

Greg slowed to ford Bobcat Creek. The water splashed up and I tightened my grip as he bumped and slid over the creek bed. He geared down to chug up the hill, then stopped at the gate.

"You get it."

I climbed off and unlatched the gate, swinging it open, and then waited for him to drive through before latching it and hopping back on. I was barely seated when the FourTrax leapt forward, heading for a lone tree in the middle of the field.

Greg pulled my strike box away from the tree and paced off the pitching distance. He set down the bucket of balls. "Pitch from here."

Greg tossed the ball to Grandad and started putting on his catcher's gear. Grandad threw a few easy ones, to help me warm up. "Step out," he said. "Your stride foot should point down so you land on your toes." Then he tossed the ball to Greg and said, "Let's go."

Greg stood behind the strike box and threw me the ball. "Come on, Joey. Knock my teeth out." He squatted and put his mitt up.

I squinted at Greg, imagining a batter in front of the box. I pulled back, lifted my knee, and threw. The ball hit the corner of the strike box and rolled to a stop ten feet away. Darn.

Greg was on his back, laughing like a hyena. "Oh man! Oh boy!"

I spat and grabbed another ball, kicking the dirt. "You're rolling in llama poop," I said.

Grandad stepped toward me. "Just throw it, JT. Every batter has a strike zone. Just find it and throw through it."

Greg stopped laughing and pasted a big cheesy grin on his face. At least that grin gave me something to aim at.

Grandad told me to bring my knee to hip height and keep my glove and shoulder in line with the target. I kicked the dirt again, pulled back, and threw. Right through the strike box and into Greg's mitt.

"Ho!" shouted Grandad. "Attaboy!"

Pitch after pitch I threw. Some were right on, and some weren't. My arm started to ache. After four balls in a row, Grandad said, "You just walked that guy."

"Yes, sir." I kicked the dirt.

"Now strike out the next one."

I squeezed my biceps, trying to find a shred of energy in the muscle.

Greg decided to act smart. He stood in front of the box, gripping the bat. "If I hit, you have to chase it," he said. He pulled the bat past his ear. Greg could hit farther than anyone I knew. He was famous all over Fireweed for being able to bat like Alex Rodriguez and pitch like Roger Clemens.

I sighed. I sure didn't want to run after the ball, but my legs had more energy than my arms. I threw: Strike one.

Grandad smiled and glanced toward the tree.

I pitched again: Strike two.

Grandad clapped his hands once, rubbed them together, then crossed his arms.

Greg whacked the mud and took his stance. He was concentrating now.

I pitched again. Greg swung a huge, powerful swing. And he missed.

Nothing but air. He groaned and rolled his eyes and smacked the barrel of the bat into his palm. Then he grinned. "Nice pitching, pip-squeak."

Grandad nodded at me. "That it is."

"I'll get you tomorrow," Greg said, holding out his hand.

I shook it. "Not if I get you first."

Just then Dad was at the fence, the packer herd behind him. He parked the FourTrax and opened the gate. "Here they come," I said.

Grandad turned. His eyes lit up as he waved at Dad.

"Want to call them in, Pop?" Dad hollered.

"Come, llamas," Grandad sang. "Come, llamas. Come, llamas."

Forty graceful necks straightened, forty pairs of curved ears perked forward. Cream-colored, rose-colored, tan, chocolate, gray, spotted, and freckled llamas. The packer herd. They walked straight to Grandad, humming hello. Most of these packers were older than me, and some were as old as Greg. The llamas in this herd had walked hundreds of miles across the mountains the past summer. They were resting this spring, but next year these females would be having crias. Maybe one of those would be the second llama in my herd.

They whiffled Grandad's hands, his chest, and his cheeks as he petted each one. "Hello, Sammy. Hello,

Tessa. Good morning, Blondie, Flo, Molly." Blue, the guard, went to the knoll and stood scanning the field, snorting white puffs into the air. Dad waved and rode back to the barn, and Greg and I collected our stuff. The sun was coming up on what looked like a great day. I grinned the whole drive home.

Greg put the FourTrax away while Grandad and I checked on Snow and her cria.

"Isn't he a beauty, Grandad?" I asked, pointing at the lump of black fur next to Snow.

"Yes sir, he's a real . . . a real . . ." Grandad staggered away from the stall. He grabbed the wall and fell to his knee on the sawdust. He coughed, trying to catch his breath.

"Grandad?" I ran to his side. "You okay?"

He put his hand on his thigh and sighed. "I'm fine, fine," he whispered. "I believe I'll just set a spell while you check the rest of the dams."

He grabbed my shoulder and I set my feet as he stood, leaning on me. His jacket was covered with straw and llama dung. "Should I go get you a pill?" I knew he took an extra pill sometimes. But I'd never seen him fall down like that. "Should we rest?"

"No, let's finish up." He coughed again and waited. "Then we'll go in."

So he sat on the bench panting while I ran and checked the stalls and refilled water buckets.

Then with my arm slung around Grandad's waist,

we slowly made our way toward the house. He leaned heavily on me, and I had to step sideways to keep my balance.

"Are you all right?"

"Sure, JT, sure," he said. But he didn't look all right, no matter what he said.

"Are you feeling sick?"

"Not sick . . . JT." He coughed again, like he was trying to clear his throat.

The house seemed to be a mile away. Our feet shuffled across the half-frozen mud. I wanted to shout for Greg or Dad or Mom to come and help, to come and see what was wrong, but I knew they wouldn't hear me. "Want me to get Dad?"

"No." Grandad's voice came out all gravelly, from way back in his throat. "Let's just get it worked out, you and I."

I grabbed him tighter. The sun was nearly full now, making the fence and grass and roof sparkle with frost. "That's some cria," I said, so I didn't have to listen to his gasping breaths.

"He's a . . . beauty."

Just thinking of Elmo again made my heart jump—my own llama. Someday my own herd. "Maybe I'll train him to guard like Sentry."

Grandad inhaled like he just came up from underwater, then bent over, coughing.

"Come on, Grandad." Don't fall again, I said to myself.

He straightened up and I saw saliva at the corner of his mouth. He swiped at it with the back of his hand, then started shuffling again.

Come on, Grandad, I thought. I held him tight around the waist as he leaned on my shoulder. Come on.

When we reached the porch, I grabbed his belt and held it as he struggled up the steps. He leaned his head on the door. When I opened it, we stumbled into the mudroom and landed on the bench with a crash. I pulled off his boots and opened the kitchen door. "Mom, something's wrong with Grandad."

Mom looked up from her coffee. She picked up the wall phone and dialed the big barn. "It's Turre," she said into the mouthpiece, then hung up. "Where is he, Joey?"

"In the mudroom." My throat was burning like I'd swallowed a hot coal. "He fell down. And he could hardly walk back from the barn."

Dad burst into the mudroom, panting. His voice got loud, like when I was in trouble. "What happened, Pop?"

I made a hot mud just for something to do, but my hands were shaking so much that I spilled coffee on the counter. Dad hurried to the cupboard, got Grandad's bottle of pills, and went back to the mudroom. "Is he sick, Mom?"

Mom sighed. "Well, he's old, Joey. Eighty-six is pretty old."

"It's not that old." I swiped at the mess with a washcloth, then threw it in the sink. I watched the brown liquid drip from the corner and slide down the drain.

Greg walked in and took my cup. "Did you know we start dying the moment we're born?" He took a big drink.

"Shut up, Greg," I said. "Grandad's sick."

Greg frowned. "Is it his heart again?"

I looked at Mom. "What's wrong with his heart?"

"Greg." Mom used her *stop it now* voice.

"What?" I said. "Tell me." I thought of his trips to the clinic, always on days when the specialist came on the mail plane. Grandad called them checkups.

Greg refilled my cup with milk, stirred in some honey, and handed it back to me. "I stopped by to see your new cria. Have you told Mom about his star?"

Then I remembered Elmo and my heart squeezed again. "Have you seen the cria yet?" I asked Mom. "Black. With a white star on his head."

Mom nodded, watching the mudroom door. "Dad's in there with Grandad. You might see if they need any help, Greg."

"Sure," Greg said, crossing the kitchen floor in three steps.

She kept her eyes on the door. I thought she hadn't heard me. Then she said, "White star's supposed to be a good sign."

"That's what Grandad said. He let me have him." I told her about pulling the legs and the little bleats Elmo made as he sucked his first breath. "Grandad said Elmo's a beauty—a fine start to my herd. I'm to take care of him, feedings, shots, training, everything, and then when I've done well by him, I get another one. That's what Grandad said."

"Works too hard," Mom said, looking past me. "I wonder if I should go out there."

"What's wrong with Grandad's heart?"

She sighed. "Basically, it's getting worn down. It doesn't work like it used to."

"Should you call the doctor?"

"Dad would have told us if he needs the doctor. I'm sure he just needed his medicine."

The door opened and Dad came in sideways, Grandad's arm across Dad's shoulder, then Grandad, and Greg holding him up on the other side.

"I'm in the pink again, boys," Grandad said, trying to pull his arms away. Dad and Greg wouldn't let go. They pivoted like a goofy line dance and started across the kitchen floor toward the hallway. Any other day they could have been joking around, faking high kicks like cheerleaders. But not today.

I jumped up and ran ahead to our room. I folded back the comforter on Grandad's bed.

They set Grandad down and stepped back.

"You feeling better, Pop?"

"Sure, sure." Grandad swiped his mouth again. "Time for my beauty rest is all."

I grinned. He sounded almost normal again. *"Grandad."*

Grandad smiled and put his hands on either side of my head. "Learn all you can at school. Bye for now." He leaned his head back on his pillow. Grandad was not pink at all—he was gray.

We turned off the light and returned to the kitchen. Dad asked me what happened and I told him how we were checking the dams and Grandad fell and how he was coughing and could barely walk from the barn to the house.

"Do you think he should see the doctor again, Robert?" Mom asked.

"You know how he feels about that," Dad said.

"That's stupid," Greg said. "If a doctor would help, why wouldn't he want to see one?"

"At this point, I don't know what the doctor would be able to do." Mom glanced at me. "Besides, he's not sure how much help he wants."

"What's that mean?" Greg was starting to get mad, like getting mad would make it any better. "He's just giving up?"

I felt like ice water was running down my back.

"No, I didn't say that. No one's saying that." Mom sighed. "But he's eighty-six and Grandma's been gone a long time. . . . A body gets tired after a while."

"We all know he wants this thing to just run its course. It's his decision." Dad stood up. "We try to respect it."

"Respect what?" I asked. "What thing?"

Dad took my elbows in his strong hands and looked up at me. "Joey, do you remember running the traplines with Nicky before Christmas?"

I nodded. Six days snowmobiling in the mountains with Nicky and his dad, checking fox traps.

"Grandad had an episode. He didn't want to stay in the hospital, but the doctor ran some tests. He was pretty sure Grandad had a heart attack."

I gulped. "Oh."

"We probably should have told you sooner—your mother and I just didn't want you to worry. Now, no one's saying he'll have another one, but we have to be careful. If you think Grandad needs help, I want you to run get me or Mom or Greg, okay?"

A lump burned in my throat. I swallowed and nodded. "Okay."

Dad stood up. "Okay. Greg, get started mucking the barn. I'll finish taking the herds out."

I followed Dad out past the small barn, where the dams stayed with their crias. The packers were already out, and so were the two sires. Tumtum and Buck had to be separated so they didn't fight, and still they sometimes jumped fences to get at each other or a female. I hadn't even tried to handle them yet—they scared me. So the bachelors, guards, and yearlings were left—they'd finished their morning grain and were anxious to get outside.

I loved to help take the herds from the barn to the fields, but I wasn't big enough to do this chore alone yet.

They wouldn't come when I called. They wandered away or just looked at me. One time a bachelor even knocked me down.

Dad opened the guard stalls and called, "Come, llamas; come, llamas. Let's go." They stepped into the aisle and followed him. As Sentry walked by, I climbed on his back for a ride. I watched the llamas crowd each other, trying to get close to Dad but never in front of him.

Dad opened the gate and walked through, calling them out across the mud and brown grass. Sentry immediately snorted at our sheep, urging them close together. Kinnaman Ranch was a llama ranch, but we kept a dozen sheep so the llamas could learn to guard them. Sheep farmers across the country and Canada paid thousands of dollars for a trained guard llama, and Kinnaman Ranch's third-year guards were the bravest of them all.

I slid off Sentry's back to the ground. Usually I liked to imagine a hundred champion llamas following me, ready to be sold. But that day my heart just wasn't in it. My mind was muddled like thick soup, with phrases like "eighty-six" and "heart attack" floating around in it. I followed Dad back to the barn, then rode to school. Early, for once.

4

After school Nicky and I rode together to tryouts. At the field, the Eagles were standing around. I squeezed my mitt shut, open, and shut again.

"Hey, JT. How many times do you think Coach Ben will spit?"

"Ten."

"No way. At least twenty."

Just then, Coach Ben turned, spat on the ground, and said, "Kinnaman, Turner. Good to see you back."

We nodded. Coach Ben was huge. He was Fireweed's police officer and knew everyone by name. He picked up his clipboard and spat again. Nicky bumped me and whispered, "Two dozen."

"Boys, welcome to the Eagles. I believe you all know each other. We have Bo Brickland back as our pitcher." He nodded at Bo, who grinned at every single player. "And Asher, our power hitter from last season," Coach continued. Asher nodded and turned pink. I liked Asher.

Coach stood at the dugout and got out a pen. "Let's throw the ball. Pair off."

Nicky grabbed a ball and I put on my mitt. We threw high, low, grounders, screamers. When I thought Coach was looking at me, I wound up and pitched to Nicky. The ball popped into Nicky's glove. "Hey!" he yelled.

"Kinnaman!"

I ran to Coach. "Yes, sir?"

"Thought I told you to throw."

"I was, sir. That was a fastball."

"I know what that was. So you think you're a pitcher now?"

I swallowed. "Well, yes sir. I've been practicing since last season."

Coach spat. That was three. Then he looked at me from my feet to my cap. "Have you, now? Is Greg working with you?"

"A little." I nodded. "I'm getting pretty good."

"We'll have to see about that." He spat again. Four. "Get out to the mound."

Coach called seven kids out to join me. Allan put on the catcher's gear and squatted behind home plate.

We had six pitches each. I tried to remember everything Grandad told me, but without the strike box it was hard to tell how close I was coming. Sometimes Allan had to reach for them, and sometimes he didn't. Coach eliminated four boys. Six more pitches. He eliminated one more. Bo, Miles, and I stood on the mound. We took turns pitching again. "Okay," Coach finally said. He wrote something on his clipboard.

I didn't see what he wrote, but it didn't matter. I did great. I knew it.

When I got home, I parked the FourTrax, checked on Elmo, and ran through the mudroom. "Grandad!" I yelled. I ran down the hall. Then I stopped, remembering, and peeked into our room. Grandad looked like he hadn't moved all day. I forgot everything I'd wanted to tell him about tryouts and just stared at him for a while. He was on his back, mouth hanging open, snoring softly. I wondered if he always looked like that when he was asleep.

I made a sandwich, grabbed my fishing pole and survival kit, and hiked out to Wolf Creek, which had thawed three weeks before. I planned to fish a little and watch the water drift by. But this late in spring, snowmelt made the creek swirl and churn, and my thoughts rushed along just like the water, too many and too jumbled to sort out: Elmo, baseball, Grandad's heart.

I leaned my pole against a tree, tied my tackle box to a branch, and checked my survival kit. I'd made it in school—poncho, pocketknife, bear bells, matches, candle, space blanket, granola bars, Band-Aids, glow sticks. Dad put an emergency flare in mine, too. Everything you might need to survive in the woods. I rolled it up in a canvas sheet and tied it with nylon rope. You had to be prepared, Grandad always said. The wilderness didn't offer second chances. I always carried the kit with me.

I started hiking up the mountain, heading for the special place I went when I needed to think. On the second ridge, I turned off the road at the salmonberry bush and continued up a steep trail. Soon I saw the corner of Kinnaman Tree House, jutting out among the branches.

I climbed up the ladder, pushed on the trapdoor, and crawled inside, remembering the first time I saw the tree house, last year.

It seemed like we'd been tromping up the trail forever that evening. My legs were tired, but Grandad had promised me a big surprise. Finally he pointed at the limbs above my head and said, "There!"

I couldn't see anything but trees and birds. I took a few steps closer, then sucked in my breath and whistled.

"I built this when your uncle was a boy," he said. It was a real tree house. Not a platform or a rickety thing slapped together. A solid floor and four walls. We climbed the ladder.

There were windows in every wall, and a railed

porch on the valley side, where I could see our whole ranch and beyond. Grandad was saying, "You can see to the inlet on a clear day."

"This is so cool," I said. Grandad understood when I said 'cool.' He didn't say 'I'm not cold,' like my parents did.

"It's yours, JT. A boy your age needs a private place to just *think.*"

"Amen," I said. It was a shelter, a place to put stuff, a place where I wouldn't get rained on or yelled at or badgered to do chores.

"If you keep it nice, it'll last another generation," he said.

I laughed. It was already as old as Uncle Del. How could it last much longer?

"You're not to the age where you think about holding on to things, JT, but someday you will be, and maybe this'll be a thing you'll want to hold on to."

I didn't get what he meant by that, but I liked how he thought I would get it someday, even if I was the youngest Kinnaman, the end of the line.

Today I noticed that the tree house was in need of repairs. Some nails were creeping out of the floorboard, and the trapdoor squeaked. I would try to remember to tell Grandad about it when he was feeling better. Maybe we could have another one of our work days—where we hammered nails and oiled hinges and weather-sealed the wood, then played checkers afterward.

I opened the wood chest and took out a package of graham crackers. Grandad and I liked to break our crackers apart and bet the pieces in a poker game. I leaned on the windowsill and munched a cracker. When fewer thoughts swirled around in my mind, I hiked down the mountain and took up my spot on the creek. The water appeared to be moving a little more slowly now that the sun was slanting toward the west.

I dug a worm and loaded my hook and spent the rest of the afternoon coaxing rainbow out of the creek. I pictured Grandad snoring in our bedroom, gurgling like the water. I hoped all he needed was a nap. I hoped he could feel better soon, and not fall down anymore or have another heart attack or worse. When the sun dipped behind the mountain, I strung my fish on a line and headed home.

5

As I kicked off my boots in the mudroom, dinner smells drifted in—rabbit stew, yeast rolls, apple pie. My stomach rumbled. I cleaned my fish, wrapped them in waxed paper, and put them in the refrigerator. Mom was at the stove.

"Joey, wash up and set the table," she said.

I washed my hands and laid out bowls and spoons, then sneaked down the hall and looked into my bedroom. Grandad was in his recliner. His eyes were open.

I let my breath out and rushed over to him. "Do you feel better?"

He flinched and looked up at me.

"Grandad?" I touched his arm. He covered my hand with his. I loved his hands—rough skin, gnarled knuckles, wrinkles and veins and brown spots—work hands.

"Are you hungry?" I asked. A tear slipped from his eye. I patted his arm. "Don't be sad, Grandad. It's only rabbit stew."

Grandad wiped his eye and smiled. "JT, my boy."

I loved being Joseph Turre Kinnaman, his namesake. Seeing him cry made my own throat close up. "What, Grandad?"

"I love you."

"And I love you," I said.

He winked his watery blue eye, real slow, and said, "Then let's eat. My stomach's chewing on my backbone."

If you were to ask me, his stomach never let go of his spine long enough to get anything in it. He hardly ate dinner. But he laughed at Greg's jokes and listened to Dad's plans for a new barn. And he wasn't as gray.

I brought my homework to the table and started writing a paper about the Denali wood frog, Mount McKinley's only amphibian. This tiny frog—an inch long—freezes solid every winter, then thaws out in the spring and goes hopping around just like normal.

We all stayed at the table with Grandad—even Greg, who usually tinkered in the machine shed, up to his elbows in grease—until bedtime.

Grandad sat with his legs crossed, hands in his lap.

His hair was sticking out, so I smoothed it over toward his ear. He winked at me.

I took that to mean he was going to be fine, no matter what people said.

I wrote my spelling words and worked ahead in math, and finally Grandad said he was ready for bed. We jumped up to help him. Dad and Greg got him down the hall and into our bedroom.

"Joey, why don't you and Greg swap rooms for the night," said Dad.

"No way," I said. "I can help him if he needs it."

"For crying out loud," Grandad said, fumbling with the buttons on his shirt. "I'm no *in-val-id.*"

I unbuttoned his shirt, then helped him take it off. His chest showed his ribs. White chest hair hung limp from his skin. I buttoned his pj top.

Dad sighed.

"Dad!" Greg said under his breath. "Joey sleeps like the dead!"

I kicked Greg and he flinched. "I want to stay in here tonight," I said.

"What if—?" Dad asked.

"We'll be fine, Robert," croaked Grandad, in a voice so loud it made me jump. "I'll send the boy if I need to. I suspect all I really need is the fuss to quit."

Dad's shoulders moved down. "Okay then." He turned to me and lowered his voice. "If you need me, or get scared, I'll be right down the hall."

I snorted. "Scared? He's a grandad, not the boogey-man."

Dad looked at me until I nodded and said, "Yes, sir."

Dad and Greg left and I sat on my bed across from Grandad. He smiled at me, a small smile that barely showed his front teeth.

"Do you feel better now?" I looked at the gray of his skin, his sagging cheeks, his hunched shoulders. I couldn't remember if he had always looked this way or not. And if he hadn't, I didn't know when it was that he'd changed. But I did know this was the first time he needed help with his buttons.

He struggled with his belt and I helped him get into his pj bottoms. Then he lay down and pulled his feet onto the bed.

With a sigh he leaned back, his head making a tiny dent in the pillow. "That's more like it," he said, his voice whispery soft. "A pillow is a small, good thing to have." He coughed again. "Why don't you pray tonight, JT?" He looked at the ceiling. "And forgive me, Lord, if I fall asleep before he's finished."

I bowed my head and thanked God for Elmo, for the health and safety of our family, and again for our health. I said, "Thank you for making Grandad well." But Grandad didn't even hear that part. When I looked up, his jaw was slack and his breathing was deep and rattling.

For a while I sat there in the silvery dark and watched him sleep. I never did get to tell him about tryouts.

Long after my parents had tiptoed down the hall and Greg's door had slammed upstairs, long after the house had settled to creaking in the wind, I pulled on my jeans and boots and sneaked out to the barn.

My boots went *shhp, shhp* on the sawdust-covered cement as I walked down the aisle. A few dams were humming at each other. I shone my flashlight back and forth. There was a new cria in Bessie's stall and Dixie had hers as well.

In Snow's stall, Elmo was curled up like a fawn under the red heat lamp. His nostrils flared as he breathed in little puffs.

Snow peered at me through the dark. "It's me, JT," I said. "Just checking on the little guy."

At the sound of my voice, Elmo lifted his head. His ears swiveled toward me as he tried to sniff out what I was. "Hey, llama. Hey, Elmo," I said. "Hey."

He laid his ears back and turned toward the wall.

Snow hummed, chewing some cud she'd saved from dinner.

Then I hummed, too. I tried to hum low, in the back of my throat, like Snow's wild music.

Elmo's ears turned toward me again, and his eyes suddenly met mine. They looked like oil, reflecting light back at me.

Maybe he couldn't really see me in the dark with those newborn eyes.

But I knew he heard me.

Later, I crawled between my cold sheets and listened to Grandad's raspy breaths again. When I closed my eyes I saw Elmo's dark eyes gazing at me. Tomorrow, more crias would be born. Tomorrow we would be a bigger, stronger ranch, with new crias to raise and train and sell. And tomorrow Grandad would be feeling better.

It was just like Grandad was always saying. Life keeps on. On a llama ranch, things are always growing and changing.

6

I woke up to hear Grandad snoring softly in his bed. He hadn't budged—he was still on his back, and his mouth still hung open.

I pulled the dresser drawers out as quietly as I could, holding my breath when the floor creaked. He didn't stir. Quickly I pulled on jeans and a sweatshirt, then tiptoed out the door, closing it behind me.

I'd done it—I'd finally sneaked by him. But even as I realized it, there wasn't much victory in my heart. It didn't count if he was sick.

Dad was already at the table, dressed in his coveralls and Kinnaman Ranch cap. "Morning."

"Morning."

"I mixed up some pancake batter if you're hungry," he said. "The skillet ought to be ready."

I made a cup of hot mud and flicked water on the skillet. The droplets danced and fizzled, evaporating into steam. "It's ready." I poured on three puddles of batter.

"How were tryouts?"

"I think I did okay. Next practice we'll find out our positions."

Dad nodded. "Sleep good?" he asked, putting his empty plate in the sink.

"Yep. Grandad's still sleeping."

"Needs the rest."

"He's probably feeling better today, don't you think?"

Dad said, "Hmm."

I flipped my pancakes. "Checked on my cria last night."

"Everything look okay?"

"Yeah—he looks healthy. And Bessie and Dixie had their crias."

"You don't say! I'll check on them first thing. And you'll need to tag your cria today and start leading him around."

"I know. I'll do that after pitching practice. Grandad and I are going out to the field after breakfast."

Dad shook his head. "Maybe you should let him rest today."

I frowned. "Well, okay, but he's going to feel better."

"In any case, you'd better tend to Snow and the cria first. She'll need an extra grain feeding while she's nursing." Dad refilled his mug. I took a sip of mud, letting it warm my throat all the way to my stomach.

"Okay." I flipped the pancakes into the air one at a time, catching them on my plate. Then I smothered them with wild blueberry syrup. I made the best pancakes in the whole family. Even Grandad said so.

I gobbled them up and poured another batch. Right when I was about to flip them onto my plate, Greg came in. He grabbed a plate and stood back. "Ready!"

I laughed and scooped a pancake onto the spatula. "Aim!"

I cocked it over my shoulder.

"Fire!"

The pancake shot through the air in a tremendous arc, almost hitting the light. Greg leapt, arms stretched out, and caught it. We cracked up.

"Boys, we've got enough to do without cleaning up messes," Dad said.

We said "Yes, sir," grinning at each other.

"I'm going to feed and drive out the herds. If there's time before school, you boys muck out the barns."

Greg groaned. I groaned. Then we said "Yes, sir" again.

After Dad left, I did an awesome behind-the-back flip, and Greg didn't even have to move to catch the pancake.

Then I tried to flip one backward over my head, but I flipped it too hard; it smacked the curtain and landed on the windowsill. "I guess I don't know my own strength," I said. I picked it up and brushed the dirt off.

Greg grabbed a fork and sat down. "You're eating that one."

Elmo was nursing when I poured grain into Snow's hopper. She stepped over him and dove into her grain, chomping and snorting. Elmo staggered after her, bleating for his breakfast. He hooked up again and they both concentrated on filling up.

In the shop I found a new green tag, #121—green because Elmo was Snow's offspring—and I wrote the number on Elmo's record card. Then I got the tag gun and swabbed it with rubbing alcohol. I washed my hands and cleaned the tag, then loaded it onto the gun and went back to the stall.

I stood beside Elmo and looked at his little black ears, hardly bigger than my pointer finger. They curved in at the tips. Elmo's ear was so soft and thin, the tag gun seemed more like a bazooka.

"Hold still," I said. I squirted iodine on his ear. I positioned the gun so the tag was in front and the clip was in the back. "Time to get your ear pierced." I held my breath.

Elmo shook his head, splattering iodine all over the stall and all over me. He stepped away and I stepped toward him and he stepped away again. I swung my leg over his neck and held his head with my thighs.

I got the tag in place—toward the bottom and outside of his ear, away from any major blood vessels. I put my finger on the trigger and squeezed.

Something hit me from behind and I went sprawling into the sawdust.

"Hey!" Spitting straw, I turned around to see Snow nuzzling Elmo, who had shoved his head in the corner like he was trying to escape through a crack. Snow stomped as I crawled toward the door.

I put the tag gun away and washed the iodine off my arms. I was leaning over the stall, watching Snow whiffle and hum at Elmo, when Greg came by. He saw me brushing straw from my shirt and started laughing. "She nailed you, didn't she? Don't you know you're supposed to take the dam out to the corral before you tag?"

"I forgot," I mumbled.

"They get upset when they think you're picking on their babies," he said.

"He didn't cry," I said.

Greg stepped into the stall and lifted Elmo's newly tagged ear. "Good position. It's bleeding a little, though. Better put some more iodine on it. And hurry up."

Snow saw me coming and started swaying, ready to butt me again. "It's okay," I sang. I remembered the wild music from the night before and tried to hum. She stepped back but kept swaying.

I petted Elmo's neck. He flinched but stood still.

"Sorry, Elmo. I had to. It won't hurt for long." I checked his ear and wiped a drop of blood onto my jeans.

I squirted iodine under the tag. Elmo shook his head like a dog, and brown spots dotted my face and hands again. I sighed and patted his neck. "Good job, llama."

7

By the time I'd washed the iodine off and Greg and I had cleaned the small barn, it was time for school, and I still hadn't haltered Elmo. Grandad didn't come out. I left a note on the table telling him I had practice that night. I knew he'd want to go.

After school, I wanted to get in a few pitches before practice, but Greg and I had to finish mucking the big barn while it was empty. It was hard enough to dodge grouchy pregnant dams in the small barn. Neither of us wanted to wait until Dad brought in the rambunctious yearlings and bachelors and try to clean stalls around them.

Nicky was pulling into the yard on his three-wheeler just as Greg and I were finishing. His curly hair scribbled out from under his hat and poofed over his ears. He held up an album with a baseball stamped on the front.

"Want to look at baseball cards?" Nicky never wanted to do much besides baseball. He ate off a plate painted like a baseball and had Babe Ruth, Ty Cobb, Nolan Ryan, and Derek Jeter posters in his room. He wore baseball socks and a different baseball cap every day of the week—one for each of his seven favorite teams. Today was a Yankees day.

I wiped the sweat off my forehead. "I have to halter train my cria. Wanna come?"

"Do what?" Nicky followed me to the barn.

"Snow had her baby," I said. "He's mine. He has to be haltered and led around every day to get trained right."

"Oh. Cool. I wish we had a farm."

"I don't think trapping and farming go together." I took a regular halter and a baby halter and two lead ropes from the tack room.

We walked down the aisle. "Now, don't be loud—be real quiet." I put my finger to my lips.

"That's impossible for me. My mom says my mouth is bigger than Alaska."

"She's right," I said. Nicky punched my arm. "But try anyway."

In Snow's stall, mother and baby were lying down, legs tucked along their sides.

I hung the leads over my arm and unlatched Snow's stall door. First I put Snow's halter on. She burped up some cud and chewed with one lazy eye watching me. Evidently she'd forgiven me for tagging Elmo that morning.

Then I touched Elmo's cheek and under his chin, just gently, like Grandad taught me. Slowly I lifted the halter over his muzzle, and buckled it behind his little black ears, being careful not to bump the new tag.

"Good, Elmo," I whispered, petting his neck. "Now let's try something else."

I clipped a lead rope to Snow's halter. "Nicky, wanna help? Come here."

Nicky stepped in the stall. "You think I can ride her?"

Nicky and I had spent many afternoons riding Snow around the corral the past summer. But I shook my head. "No. She just had a baby. We're taking them out to the corral for a walk."

"Oh, okay." Nicky looked disappointed. He loved to ride our llamas, even though he often landed on his rear in the grass. But he was always ready to do it again.

"If we can catch Sentry, we'll ride him a little later. Take Snow's lead rope. Hold it right under her chin so you can steer her head." I showed Nicky how to put his hands, coiling the extra rope in one hand. "Stand." Snow grunted and stood, one leg at a time, pushing her rear half up first, then her front. She stomped as if to say, "Well? What now?"

I clipped the lead onto Elmo's halter. With a clumsy

shuffling of hooves and long legs, he stood, then pulled back with all his might. "Go on out, Nicky," I said. "Let's get them moving." I took a tighter hold of Elmo's lead rope. If he got loose, he could trip on the lead rope and break his neck.

Nicky led Snow out of the stall, and Elmo smashed himself against the doorway trying to stay next to her. "Easy, llama," I crooned, gently pulling him back. "Easy, Elmo. Let's go to the corral, Nicky."

We walked down the aisle, Elmo dancing at Snow's hind legs. Snow kept raising her foot and sidestepping.

I followed Elmo's quick movements as best I could, trying to stay at his head. It was important to stay at a llama's head when you wanted him to mind. Also I was afraid Snow would get irritated and kick him, or kick me. Elmo jerked his head back and forth, trying to shake off the strange feel of the halter.

Inside the corral, Nicky led Snow in a wide circle. I tried to get Elmo to follow a pace behind, but the harder I pulled, the harder he pulled. He wanted to be by his mother and I wasn't convincing him of anything else. Soon I was walking close to the fence, with Elmo next to me and Snow right next to Elmo. Nicky was chattering about the stats for the entire league: win-loss records, the batters, the pitchers. "I don't know, I don't think the Chargers' pitcher throws good junk. I mean, he's got a few moves, but have you seen his fastball?"

Then before I knew it, Snow was pushing me along the fence. A board hooked my shirt and I felt a splinter poke my shoulder. "Nicky! Pull her to the middle!" I shouted.

"Oh! Whoops!" But before Nicky could do anything, Snow took aim to slam into me. I unclipped Elmo's lead and slipped between the boards of the fence just in time. Elmo ducked under his mother, and Snow shoved her side against the fence. I almost got smashed.

"Snow!" I hollered. She turned and looked at me like she hadn't done a thing.

Nicky threw his hands in the air, trying not to laugh. "Sorry."

I picked the sliver out of my shoulder. Llamas were smart; I loved that about them. You always had to be thinking. "Let's leave them here and go pitch for a while. Then we'll go see if we can catch Sentry."

We latched the gate and ran out to the south field, but Tex and the bachelors were there. Tex was one of our bravest and toughest llamas, a big red guy standing a head taller than Grandad. He was a guard like Sentry and had defended our llamas from coyotes, wolves, and probably more animals we didn't know about. He had scars on his legs and a chunk missing from his ear to prove it. Tex always guarded the bachelors, our most valuable herd. The cash crop, Grandad called them, because we sold most of them every fall. Dave, a chocolate third-year, perked his ears at us and took a step.

"Dave has the makings of a good guard," I said, watching him.

"How can you tell?"

"He walks toward anything unusual. Most llamas run."

"How do you teach them to guard?"

"You don't. It's something they're born with. He'll follow Tex around for a while longer, then go to the sheep field with Sentry, then get sold to a farm."

"Are you ever sad when they go?"

"Not really. That's what they're for. Are you sad when you skin a fox and sell the pelt?"

Nicky laughed. "No."

"It's like that."

We played catch in the south field for a while, but it wasn't any fun. "Want to ride?" I finally asked.

"Sure!" Nicky dropped his mitt.

We hopped the short inside fences over to the sheep field. As soon as Sentry saw me, he walked over. He stopped and peered down at me, his eyelashes glinting orange in the sun.

"Cush," I said, standing on tiptoe to make myself tall. Sentry blinked.

"Cush." I pushed his shoulder. A llama didn't respect short people or short animals. That was why we had to keep the sheep. It took time for a llama to learn to like sheep well enough to protect a flock. "Cush!"

Nicky snorted.

"Let me stand on your back, Nick," I said.

"Aw, JT, really?"

"Yeah. Just for a second. Get on your hands and knees."

Nicky got down. I stood on his back and stretched up as tall as I could, putting my hand flat toward the ground. *"Cush."*

Sentry eyed me, then slowly lowered himself to the ground, bending his knees and kneeling, then lowering his hindquarters.

"You go first," I said.

Nicky climbed onto Sentry's back and grabbed hold of the thick fiber along Sentry's neck.

"Stand," I said, lifting my palm to my chest.

Sentry stood. I walked a few steps away. "Come, llama." Sentry took one step, then turned and went the other way. I ran to get beside his head. "See if you can get him to run," Nicky said.

"He won't. Not unless there's danger."

"Then scare him. I want him to run."

"Nope."

"Get on with me, then."

I shook my head. "He'll just sit down. Grandad says a llama won't ever carry something too heavy for its back. They sit down, and won't get up. Not like horses. You can overload a horse and the dumb thing will just walk until his back breaks."

"Does your brother ever ride him?"

"Too big," I said.

Nicky sat up tall. "When will we be too big?"

"I don't know. Hey, let me have a turn. Sentry, cush."

This time Sentry knelt immediately, happy to be

relieved of his load. I climbed on and told Sentry to get up. He stood. Then his whole body stiffened as he stretched his neck up, sniffing the air. Suddenly he took off like he heard a gunshot, giving an alarm bark that made the other guards run together. I grabbed wildly for a handful of hair as he galloped back to his herd. He grouped them into a tight circle, grunting and humming and butting at them to move them closer together, sheep in the middle, guards in a tight ring around them.

Nicky came running. "See? You knew how to make him run," he whined.

I swung a leg over and slid off Sentry's back. "No, he smells something."

"What?"

"Don't know."

Sentry looked this way and that, snorting.

"Let's ride him some more," Nicky said.

I shook my head. "I don't want to distract him. It's almost time for practice, anyway." I glanced at Sentry one more time. He stood rigid, scanning the base of the mountain.

"Oh yeah." Nicky happily returned to his favorite subject as we walked back. "I can't wait. I bet I'll be lead scorer this year. I've been practicing with the bat I got for Christmas. Did I tell you about it?" Nicky started describing his bat. It was probably the thousandth time he'd told me, but I let him talk. I didn't know what

Sentry was smelling or if he really sensed danger, but I wasn't going to bother him, in case there really was something out there.

At practice, Coach gathered us in to read off our positions. I watched the bleachers for Grandad, but he wasn't there. "Brickland, you'll start as pitcher." I held my breath. "Kinnaman, you've earned yourself a spot as relief pitcher. Miles, you keep practicing. Remember, boys, this can change. Work hard—I notice effort."

I turned to look at Nicky. He gave me a thumbs-up and grinned. We popped fists and high-fived. "You go, man!" he said, as I looked at the bleachers again. Where was Grandad? I was itching to tell him I was the Eagles' new relief pitcher. Me. JT Kinnaman.

"That's it, Eagles," Coach yelled. "Next practice tomorrow night. If you're late, you run."

Bo Brickland stepped in front of me. "You won't get much playing time, you know," he said.

"Coach will play me if he needs me."

"He won't need you," Bo said, sneering.

Nicky shoved his way between Bo and me. "Let's go, JT."

I tried to think of something to say, something that would make Bo look stupid. But my tongue was all tied up.

Grandad would tell me sometimes it's better not to say anything at all.

By the time I put Snow and Elmo back in their stall, I was late for dinner—salmon steaks and lemon rice—but Dad filled a plate for me as I untied my cleats.

"How'd it go today?" Grandad asked.

"I got relief pitcher."

"Attaboy!" said Grandad. "We'll get some more practice in."

"Not just yet, Pop," Dad said. "Let's get you feeling better, shall we?"

Grandad clunked his coffee cup on the table. "I've never been one to sit in a chair while life passes by, Robert. And there will be no more fuss about it."

I looked around the table. After an awkward silence, Greg whacked my back and Dad said, "Pitcher! I'll be!"

No one said anything else about pitching practice. When Grandad spoke that way, that was it.

8

For the rest of that week and the next, the Eagles practiced every night. Mom and Dad didn't come to practice, but they promised to make the games. The year before, Grandad had come to practice—he even sat in the dugout with me sometimes—but he wasn't coming so far this season, either. Greg was busy with his last high school season before graduating, so I didn't see him unless we mucked out the barn together.

Coach really wanted to win the championship this year. Apparently he thought the way to get it was drill. So my team ran the bases, ran the field boundaries, did push-ups, batted left, batted right, and fielded pop-ups, grounders, and fouls. I pitched so much I felt like my shoulders were getting lopsided.

Every morning before school I checked on Elmo and Snow. Every day there were more crias, sometimes two or three a day. Then after baseball practice, I'd come home, do my chores, do my homework, and go train Elmo. I put on his halter, led him around, and talked to him so he would learn my voice. Then I would drag my tired self into the house, play a game of checkers with Grandad, and go to bed thinking of lots of things: Grandad's cough that seemed to be getting worse every day, Elmo growing bigger right before my eyes, and what it would be like to pitch a no-hitter.

Day by day the minutes of sunlight increased. I watched the sun rise from the window of the school-house and watched it set over the ball field. The long days were coming. The ground was thawing and the ice on Kamchatka Lake split open. Breakup was officially here.

Thursday night after practice Coach told us to take a knee. "Eagles, Saturday is our opening game. As you know, there's a pizza party and a trophy for the team that shows the most spirit and wins the most games. We're ready to get out there and give it our best. Take to-morrow off, and meet at the park Saturday at ten o'clock. Now, put your hand in for a cheer."

We yelled *"One, two, three—go, Eagles!"* and my stomach fluttered all the way home. I didn't see how I could wait two whole days for the opening game.

Saturday morning I was awake before I even opened my eyes. My mind went from dreaming about catching a king salmon to the sudden realization that today was the day. Game day.

I dressed as fast as I could, stuffed my feet into my boots, and ran out to check on Elmo.

Grandad was in the small barn, looking over the crias. He had his blue coveralls on and his work boots laced up.

"Grandad!" I said in surprise.

"Good morning to you, too!" he answered. He broke into a fit of coughing.

"What're you doing out here?"

He walked slowly to Dixie's stall. "Well now, I've got a ranch to run, don't I? And isn't it somebody's first game?" He patted his pocket and I noticed he had his red pocket protector today. Red was our team color.

I grabbed him around the waist in a hug. "I'm checking on my herd, too."

Snow nickered at me when I approached, now used to my visits. Elmo lifted his head and sniffed. To my eye, he was bigger than he'd been the day before. I poured grain into the hopper and checked his umbilical cord. It was shriveled and black, like a piece of jerky. It should be ready to fall off in another day or two. His tag piercing was healing well, too—no signs of infection. I patted his head and rubbed his neck but stopped when Elmo turned away. Grandad said never to follow a llama to pet it. Then they never learn to come to you.

I clipped the halter on Snow and led her out of the barn. She kept turning her head, looking for Elmo. "I'll go get him. Don't worry, he's coming," I said, letting her loose in the back corral. She walked into the weak spring sunshine, lay down, and rolled in the dirt.

I went back to get Elmo and this time he danced around me in tight circles all the way to the scale. I set him on it, and he jumped off. I set him on again, holding his head down with the lead rope. He pranced and tried to chest-butt me. "You're going to need some work if you intend to be a pack llama," I told him. "Packers are *calm.*" He waggled his ears. I set him on the scale again and held his throat with my palm. Sixteen pounds. I wrote his weight on his card. I wanted to keep careful records; any Kinnaman knew that was key to running a good llama ranch.

I led him out to the corral, and when he saw his mother he gave a tremendous bawl, as though he hadn't seen her in days. I took off the halter and pushed his rump—he staggered and ran to her, bumping into her leg. "See you later, llamas."

I met Dad going out of the barn. "Hey, Dad."

"Morning. How's your stock looking?"

"Good. He weighs sixteen pounds now."

Dad shook his head. "Still tiny."

"Yeah, but he's strong."

"Has he lost his cord yet?"

"Not yet."

"Watch it for infection."

"I am."

"Are you leaving them in the corral?"

"Yeah. I think Elmo could use the fresh air. And it's warm enough."

Dad shook his head. "Then you'd better put them out with Tex and the bachelors in the back field. Greg saw bear tracks along the fence. And take Bessie and Lolly and their crias out, too."

"Okay."

"We'll see you at the big game. Are you ready?"

I grinned. "Batter up."

❖❖

In the kitchen Mom was frying eggs and sausage. She wore a red flannel shirt and red baseball cap.

She set a cup of hot mud and a plate in front of me. "Hungry?"

"Starved." I smelled the sausage patties on my plate. "Reindeer?"

Mom nodded. "Nothing but the best."

"Is this Dasher or Dancer?"

Mom smiled. "Could be either one. We ate Rudolph last week."

"Mother!" Greg said, walking in. "You're going to

warp that boy. We'd never eat Santa's reindeer. Unless they wandered onto our property, that is." He gave me a noogie before pouring a cup of coffee and sitting next to me on the bench. "Ready for the game? Got your pompoms?"

"Oh, put some food in your mouth." I *was* ready, but the more I thought about it, the more nervous I got.

"Remember to pitch low. They always strike when you pitch low."

"I might not even get to pitch. I'm the relief pitcher, remember?"

"You never know."

I sighed. I wasn't sure how to get the ball over the plate every pitch, much less aim it at a low corner of the strike zone like Greg could do. I wasn't Greg.

Grandad came in from the mudroom. "Morning!"

"Turre, you sure look chipper this morning. You must be feeling better." Mom kissed Grandad's cheek.

Grandad waggled his eyebrows at Greg and me. I laughed. Grandad was crazy. Just crazy.

"I'll go along with you, JT," said Grandad. He coughed and sat down. "I'll just set a minute and I'll be ready."

Mom brought him a cup of coffee. "Are you sure, Turre?"

"Sure I'm sure."

"Greg, are you going along with Grandad and Joey?" Mom gave him a look.

"I was supposed to help Dad in the big barn this morning . . ."

Mom opened her mouth to talk, but Grandad put up a hand. "I'm fine, I tell you."

"He's fine," I said, trying to sound casual. "Well, I'd better get dressed."

Mom, Grandad, and Greg started a chant. "Go, Eagles! Go, Eagles!"

They cracked me up.

After a shower, I put on my uniform slowly—gray pants, red shirt, red belt, red socks. I put on my cap and looked at myself in the mirror, setting my mouth in a straight line. "Batter up," I muttered. I looked pretty mean.

An hour before the game, I was out in the yard, throwing the ball and catching it, waiting for Grandad. I was ready to leave *now*. My stomach was jumping and my insides turned cartwheels. I wished there was enough time to drive to the strike box and warm up. Maybe Grandad had decided to go with Mom and Dad. If I just *knew* I would get out on the ball field and do fine, the knot in my gut might go away. Where was he?

Grandad opened the mudroom door and carefully walked down the steps, holding the rail. His face was white and he was unsteady on his feet. "Ready?" he asked, smiling.

"I've been waiting for you." I wanted to ask him why he didn't look so good anymore, but I didn't. I just watched him totter toward me.

"What's the matter? Nerves getting to you?" Grandad rested one hand on my shoulder. I don't know if it was for me or for him. "Concentration is all it takes, JT. Find the zone and work through it."

"Easy for you to say," I said, kicking the dirt with my toe.

"Careful, JT" was all Grandad said. He looked right into my eyes for a minute, until I understood. Then he held up a red cap. "You need this?"

"I thought I was wearing that." I took off the cap I had on—my Kinnaman Ranch hat. "Whoops."

Grandad put the red cap on my head. "Can't ever get away from our roots, can we?"

I smiled. "Nope." I pulled the shed door open and grabbed the key from the hook. "I'm driving, okay?" I strapped my bat bag to the cargo rack, started the engine, and slowly backed up to Grandad. "Ready." I stood up and held Grandad's arm as he lifted his foot over the seat and sat down. He sighed. "Ready."

Grandad used to race Greg on four-wheelers when I was little. He'd put me on the back and we'd race through the hills. Sometimes he invented scavenger hunts. "First one back with a moose antler and a beaver-chewed stick is the winner." We would plow along logging roads and over streams.

As I drove down the gravel road and onto Fireweed's main street, past the diner, past the World War II Quonset hut medical clinic, and past the school, I wondered how long it had been since Grandad took us on a race. Or for that matter, how long it had been since Grandad drove at all.

I pulled up to the field and shut off the engine. Most of the Eagles were already there.

"JT!" Nicky waved. "Let's go, man!"

I grabbed my bat bag and started to run off. Then I stopped. Grandad was still sitting on the seat.

"Don't get lazy on me," I joked. I walked back and held out my elbow.

"Guess I can't if you won't let me." Grandad laughed and grabbed my arm. He stood and swung his foot over, stumbling back. I stayed fixed until he was steady.

"I'll help you find a spot on the bleachers, Grandad."

"I can manage. You go have a good game." He patted my shoulder.

He made his way to the bleachers, hands out a little for balance. I followed him a few steps. "Get going now," he said.

I ran out to Nicky. "Hey." We popped fists.

"Ready?"

"Sure." I looked at the Chargers, warming up in the outfield. "They don't look like much," I said in my toughest voice. I hoped I sounded tougher than I felt. Nicky laughed and backed up, holding his mitt high.

I threw him the ball. He fired it back to me. We warmed up until Coach called balls in and we ran to the dugout. I craned my neck until I could see Grandad,

Mom, Dad, and Greg on the bleachers. I hoped Grandad could see me strike somebody out today.

The game was going great—I scored a nice run in the top of the third, and by the last inning, we were up 6–2. That was when Coach spat on the ground and said, "Kinnaman! Warm up!"

I wasn't sure if I was excited or about to get sick. Probably both.

Nicky and I started throwing the ball in the bullpen. Coach came over to watch. He had a huge wad of bubble gum in his mouth. I could see flashes of pink as he talked. "Throw steady. Don't get rattled."

"Yessir." I nodded. I was already rattled.

I reminded myself I was just the cleanup guy—all I was supposed to do was get three outs. I imagined I was Cy Young, Grandad's all-time favorite pitcher, who Grandad's dad actually *saw* pitch the very first American League no-hitter. Unflappable.

A roar erupted from the bleachers when I walked onto the field. There wasn't a whole lot to do in Fireweed, so ball games always drew a big crowd when the Pipeline workers and trappers were home on weekends. The parents and folks in the stands started yelling and stamping their feet.

Suddenly it looked like the Chargers had collected all the biggest kids in Fireweed for their team.

"They look huge," I told Nicky.

"No they aren't." Nicky whacked my back. "You're just scared."

"I'm not scared," I said.

"Good."

I took the mound and threw some warm-up pitches. The catcher, Allan, couldn't seem to catch them.

"Come on, Al," I yelled after the fourth pitch got past him.

"Decent pitch!" yelled Allan.

"Batter up!" yelled the umpire.

The Chargers' batter *was* big. How he ever got in the ten-and-under league I couldn't guess. He looked old enough to shave. He pulled his bat back and glared at me for a second before his eyes focused on the ball.

I took a deep breath. I wound up and pitched.

Strike.

Grandad's voice carried over the cheers from the stands. "Attaboy!"

The batter whacked home plate, set his feet, and pulled back again.

I looked at the ball, then the batter, and pitched.

Strike.

I turned to grin at Nicky, who was playing shortstop. He gave me a thumbs-up.

The Chargers' coach came out to talk to the batter and I retied my shoe.

"Play ball!" the ump shouted.

I wound up and stepped out, imagining that I was Cy—cool as ice. A pitching machine. I imagined my teammates lifting me up on their shoulders after I held off the Chargers for a win.

The ball connected to the bat with a crack. It took me a second to find it in the air—sailing for center field. Hitch was there to make the catch for the first out. I exhaled. Two to go.

The second batter stepped into the box, prancing like a banty rooster and swinging like he was still in T-ball. I could tell by looking that he'd swing at anything.

And he did. He struck out so fast the umpire had to yell, "Next batter!" The banty rooster stomped off, kicking the fence before he slumped to his seat in the dugout.

Nicky yelled, *"You go, JT! You're the man, JT!"*

The next batter was John Ant—a friend from school. I smiled at him and then fired the fastest pitch I could. "Ball!" yelled the ump.

"Whatever," Nicky yelled.

I wound up, pointed my elbow, and let go. John smacked it to the hole between center and right and took off running. Hitch and Asher raced after it, but John was on second before Asher could throw it in.

"Keep your cool, Kinnaman," shouted Coach.

Usually the number four batter was the best, so I was ready when a big arrogant guy came out of the dugout. He sauntered up to the plate, staring at me the whole time.

"Focus," Grandad called.

I felt my stomach clench and thought for a second I might actually throw up. I shook that thought from my head.

I wound up to pitch and then heard Nicky: *"Third!"*

I checked my pitch, pivoted, and threw to Lonny on third, who almost tagged John out but missed.

The stands erupted in cheers.

"Attaboy! Good try!"

I wound up and pitched. Ball.

Second pitch: strike.

Third pitch: ball.

Fourth pitch: ball.

Coach called time and stalked out to the mound. His pink gum danced around in his mouth. "How many more you want to throw this inning, son?"

"Two." I picked up a handful of dirt.

"Then do it."

"Play ball!" shouted the umpire.

I looked at the batter's stance. He was going to wait and make sure this pitch was good. And I made sure it was—bottom right corner of the strike zone. He didn't even swing. I started to wind up for the last pitch.

"Ball!"

I stopped and looked. The batter gave me a huge grin. He sauntered all the way to first. The Eagles were too disgusted to even yell at him.

"Oh man," I said. That was a strike. I looked at Coach. He put up his hands and nodded to me to get ready for the next batter.

I threw a meat pitch, and he easily connected. Asher fielded it, but not before the runner made it to first. The next pitch was really ugly, landing in the dirt in front of home plate.

I threw two more balls. My eyes started to sting.

"Hey, JT, what're you doing?" Nicky sounded disgusted.

I walked that guy, too, and the next one. Two runs walked in. 6–4. Then Coach called me out of the game. "Take a break, son."

I slumped onto the bench. Coach sent Miles out. What went wrong?

I heard Grandad's voice behind me. "JT."

I turned and looked at him through the fence. "Hey."

"You doing your best?"

"Yeah!" I hit my mitt. "That's what makes me so mad! I'm trying. I don't know what happened. And that one call wasn't fair! That was a strike!"

"Maybe." Grandad looked at me for a second. "You do your best and you keep your head up. Nobody can ask any more of you than that." He walked back to the bleachers in a slow, crooked line.

And no one did ask any more of me. Miles pitched fine, but the Chargers were on a roll and we didn't get the third out until we were behind 6–7. We lost.

Dad and Greg told me it was a good try. Mom gave me a hug. Then Coach told us all to take a knee for a minute. "Listen up, boys," he said, but I didn't want to.

I watched parents fold up their lawn chairs and climb on their three-wheelers and four-wheelers. The forest ranger pulled into the parking lot in his green truck.

"*One, two, three—go, Eagles!*" we shouted when Coach was finished. Grandad put his arm on my shoulder and guided me toward the FourTrax. "I told your parents to go ahead without us," he said.

Mom and Dad were getting in the crummy as Greg took off on the other FourTrax with the ranger following. Grandad waved with one hand and settled on the seat behind me. I started the FourTrax and drove in low gear through town, trying not to cry.

"You did play a good game, you know," Grandad said in my ear as we drove.

"I walked three guys," I said. "We lost."

"Sure, that's true, but you struck out a few, too. And you scored a run. Look at the whole picture, JT."

"I guess."

"No guessing about it. You know what'll perk you up?"

"What?"

"A big fat slice of apple pie."

"I don't feel like it, Grandad," I said. I wanted to go home and hide in the barn.

"Too bad. Sometimes you've got to do stuff you don't feel like doing. Life keeps on keeping on, even after something bad happens, you know."

"*Grandad,*" I groaned. But there was no talking him out of it. We were going to Lou's.

9

I pulled into the gravel parking lot of Lou's Diner. Four-wheelers were parked in two rows. "Here we are!" said Grandad. "The best restaurant in town!"

I had to laugh. It was the *only* restaurant in town.

Lou's wasn't actually a diner at all, but an old house turned restaurant, with a maze of rooms tacked onto it. My favorite was the red room—the walls were sponge-painted red, the chairs were red, and the ceiling had red stars stenciled on it. Grandad let out a huge rattling cough. No matter what he said, he didn't feel well. I could tell. He reached for the wall as he walked through the diner.

We slid into a red vinyl booth and Lou brought two glasses of water. "How was the game?"

"Put up a good fight," Grandad said.

"We lost to the Chargers," I said, running my finger along my water glass.

"The season's young yet," said Lou. "You'll live. Now, what do y'all want to eat? Got grits."

"Lou, this is likely the only place in Alaska that serves grits," Grandad said, smiling.

"So I may as well serve you some. Butter or cheese on 'em?"

I made a face. "Do people really eat like that where you grew up?"

Lou drew herself up like I'd just insulted her mother. "The fine state of Mississippi, God bless it, is well known for its excellent cuisine," she said in a huff.

Grandad laughed.

"I'll have apple pie just the same," I said.

"You're missing out," warned Lou.

"A la mode, please," Grandad said. "Coffee for me and mud for the boy."

"Right-o." Lou waddled out of the room.

I looked around, hoping none of the other Eagles would come in.

"You played well for most of the game," Grandad said.

"I guess. But we still lost."

Lou brought two steaming mugs. "Plenty of milk for

you. Too much coffee'll stunt your growth, you know."
She winked.

"I'm growing, I'm growing," I said.

"Don't remind me. I remember the day your grand-daddy brought you in on his shoulder. Pie'll be right out." She hustled off again.

I stirred my hot mud and looked at Grandad. I loved how his wrinkles ran every which way, and when he laughed, they settled in all the right places. His eyes were pale blue and his eyebrows were set high on his forehead so he always looked surprised.

It was time for Grandad to start his talk. He always went over the same three things at Lou's: first cup of coffee, baseball. Second cup, good character. Third cup, following the harvest west from Wisconsin to Oregon, then hitchhiking to Alaska during the Depression. Math facts were sprinkled throughout.

"We ought to get a little more practice in," he said, sipping his coffee.

"Sure," I said. I didn't want to think about practice. Part of me wanted to quit pitching altogether. But for Grandad, there was always hope.

"Did you figure out your trouble out there?"

"Too high."

"Good." Grandad nodded. "How would you correct yourself?"

"Bring it lower. Pull down in my forearm some."

He slapped the table and laughed. "That's my boy!"

he crowed, like I'd saved the World Series or something. "I want to know your strategy for the next game."

That was what I loved about Grandad. He always wanted to hear about what *I* was thinking. "I figure I'll start low. We play the Bears next. They've got a switch-hitter I'll throw two low, then one high and inside. It ought to trick him no matter which way he goes."

Grandad winked at me. "That's the spirit."

He drained his cup and slid it to the edge of the table. "What's twelve squared?"

I grinned. "One hundred forty-four." I really dug math, just like Grandad. "What's thirteen squared?"

"One sixty-nine! A man after my own heart!" Grandad cackled again and I laughed, too.

Lou brought our pie and refilled Grandad's coffee. She waited for him to take a sip and said, "Tell me the truth, now. Have you ever tasted better coffee?"

"Heaven's finest couldn't be any better," Grandad said.

Lou nodded, satisfied, and shuffled away.

"Do you know what mettle is, JT?"

"You mean like aluminum?"

"*M-E-T-T-L-E.* It's a word to learn, son."

"What is it?"

"Character. Spirit. Courage. It takes mettle to make it in life."

I tried it out. "Mettle."

"I was fourteen when my father sat us kids down and

said there's too many kids to feed. I hopped a train car and never looked back. I'd go to a restaurant that served a dime plate dinner, and not have the dime," he said. "I'd knock on the kitchen door and ask what they might have me do to earn that dime for my dinner."

Never in my life have I had to work for my dinner, not really. It was just there. "That's smart, Grandad."

"No, that's mettle. Finding a way even if it looks like there isn't a way. I'd wash dishes, wash the car, sweep. I'd do any work they'd tell me to do, and I'd earn my dinner. There was always a way."

"Where did you sleep at night?"

"Usually I'd find a farm and ask if I could sleep in the barn in exchange for splitting wood or some chore like that. Put a little straw over my head and I was pretty snug." He smiled. "It might look hopeless, no money in your pocket, no food, and no bed. But if you keep on looking, eventually you'll see a way."

He gazed out the window, like maybe he was re-membering warm barns and train cars and diners from the old days. "Some things are harder to do than others, but a body learns to keep on. You're learning to keep on, JT."

Grandad had mettle I didn't think I had. Next to him, I was a big old chicken. But he didn't think so. Grandad had a way of doing things, like taking a loser ball game and making me feel like I'd done all right after all.

Maybe I had.

He pointed his finger and waggled it at me. "What's twelve squared?"

Did he not remember saying that already? I looked at him. He had huge circles under his eyes and his eyelids were drooping. Saliva was slipping from the corner of his mouth again. His eyes were watery, like he was about to cry. He rubbed his hair across the top of his head and said, "Where was I?"

"Mom will be wondering about us," I said, even though he hadn't talked about following the harvest yet.

"Now, that's true," Grandad said, draining his cup. He left a quarter for Lou and stood, then leaned on the table for a moment, holding on with both hands. I was afraid he might fall again, but he straightened up and put on his cap and walked out, grabbing chairs for balance.

10

There was no time for back pats or babying when we got home, if I'd been looking for some. Kinnaman Ranch was in an uproar.

Greg waved at us as we pulled up. "Joey!" he yelled, grabbing the gas can. "Come help us!"

Grandad slowly stood. "What's wrong?"

"The whole bachelor herd is loose. Dad's rounding up by Bobcat Creek and Mom and the ranger are looking on the north side."

"Lord have mercy," Grandad breathed. "How'd it happen?"

"The fence must be down. We haven't had a chance to see how bad it is." Greg nodded at me. "Joey, ride the perimeter."

I nodded. "Are we tracking a bear?"

"Not yet."

"We need to secure the outside fence," Grandad said. "And get the llamas in the barn before they all get killed. Has to be bear. What else would attack like that?"

My heart dropped to my stomach as I poured gas into the FourTrax. A trained guard would charge at predators, and usually that was all it took to scare off a cowardly animal, like a coyote or a wolf. But a hungry pack or a sow grizzly with hungry cubs could be trouble. Even Tex was no match for a half-ton bear with paws the size of dinner plates and claws longer than my fingers. A bear had ripped through the fence once, and I still remembered Grandad crying over the dead llamas.

I ran to the mudroom, took off my cleats, and shoved my feet into my boots. I swapped hats again and ran back out.

"I'll get tools to patch the fence," Grandad was saying. "You boys go on. Be watchful."

I knew what Grandad meant. Our ranch was surrounded by wilderness and the scent of wandering llamas would surely draw out every carnivore with an empty belly. Wolves had taken dogs from their front yards. Moose stomped and killed people on occasion. Even bald eagles had been spotted snatching kittens, although I hadn't seen that myself. There were wolverines, wildcats, and coyotes to consider as well. Most dangerous of all, Fireweed's bears were waking up.

When I noticed the corral gate swinging open, I remembered: Elmo and Snow were with the bachelors! I ran into the small barn to be sure. "Snow!" No sign of them. My stomach clenched with fear. "Snow!"

I rode slowly on the perimeter road, calling their names and scanning the fence for sagging wire or holes. The fence was eight feet high to keep out jumping animals, like cats and caribou, and the mesh was woven tight to keep out wolves, black bears, and wolverines. I didn't see anything for miles. But then I found it—a huge gash in the fence. The wire was torn apart like it was yarn. Two-toed hoofprints—llama—were mashed in the soft earth on both sides of the fence.

I plucked a piece of brown fur from the wire and smelled it. Rank and musky—brown bear. A bear must have torn through the fence while we were away at the game. I hoped the herd was able to run away. I hoped Snow and Elmo were safe.

I pulled the edges of the gaping hole together as well as I could. It was like trying to pull the skin over a big cut. I measured the gap with my arm. It reached all the way from my fingertips to my shoulder. On the road, I went full throttle, racing back to the yard. We were in big trouble.

Dad and Greg were struggling to lead Buck and

Tumtum into the barn. The sires were jerking their heads back and dancing sideways into each other, rearing and snorting, spooked out of their minds.

Dad talked softly as they reared and spat and barked alarm calls. "Stay back, Joey," he said. Finally he got them into stalls.

"I found the hole, Dad."

"Where at?"

"West field." I showed him how big the gap measured on my arm. "It's torn maybe six feet up and all the way to the ground."

"Are you sure?"

"Yeah. Maybe a little more."

"The bachelors weren't even over there today. The yearlings were."

"Yearlings are gone, too," Greg said. "The inside fencing's torn through."

I showed Dad the fur. "Grizzly," he said, and threw it on the ground.

Grandad came out of the shed with wire cutters, gloves, and a spool of fencing wire. "There's likely another break we haven't found yet."

Dad nodded. "Maybe the bear got in at the yearlings and then came chasing through the interior fence to the bachelors."

I could see in my mind the last llama caught by a bear. Skin ripped and bloody, guts hanging from his belly.

"Joey, you go out and fix the fence. Greg, take the FourTrax and see if any llamas wandered into town. Tell people we may need help rounding them up. I'll go see if Mom's found any."

"How many have you found, Dad?" I asked.

"Three yearlings and a bachelor." He sighed. "We don't have much time—the farther they run, the more likely they'll find trouble. The yearlings and the bachelors. Lord have mercy."

Grandad gave us each a handful of halters and lead ropes. "I'll go out with JT."

"No, Pop, you would have to walk all that way. Stay by the phone in case someone sees them."

Grandad blinked and ducked his head.

"It's not that far," I said quickly. "And I could use the help. It's a big hole."

"Let's go then," Grandad said. "I'm not too old to be of use, Robert."

Dad looked at Grandad for a second, but there was no time to argue. I picked up the heavy bucket and started after Grandad.

After a few minutes, I was wishing Grandad had listened to Dad. He kept stumbling on the uneven dirt, tripping on rocks and roots. Several times he stopped at a tree, putting his palm on the white birch bark, to catch his breath. My fingers felt like they were getting sliced off from the weight of the bucket.

"Do you want to wait here while I go on and fix it?" I asked.

Grandad tipped his head sideways and looked at me in a way that told me I'd insulted him.

Then I had an idea. "Just wait here a second," I said.

I ran into the woods and found a nice-sized walking stick. "Here!" I demonstrated. "Try this, Grandad."

Grandad grinned. He took the stick and tested it. "I once tracked a bear that was fooling with my herd. Tracked him for two weeks. Shot him, too." He walked a few steps with the stick for balance. "Much better," he said. "I thank you, JT."

I flushed, feeling tall and important. "Aw, no big deal, Grandad. I think I'll run and get a stick for me, too."

"I'll get a head start on you, then." Grandad walked on, using the stick to steady his steps.

I ran back into the woods, searching for a strong limb I could use to yoke the bucket of U-nails, clippers, wire, and hammers over my shoulder, instead of holding it.

Then I screeched and jumped back. Right at my feet, under a fern, I saw a bloody carcass.

I froze. The smell of fresh blood made a metallic taste in my mouth. I listened for an animal guarding the kill. Nothing. I backed away slowly, not wanting to surprise an animal into thinking I might steal its dinner.

I knew it was one of our llamas by its white fiber and hooves—too big to be a Dahl sheep or mountain goat—but I didn't know who. The neck was folded under the body.

I clapped my hands. No crashing through the brush, no rustling leaves. Cautiously I stepped closer, then knelt down beside the llama. Blood and dirt stuck to my hands as I pulled on the neck, straining to get the head out from under the shoulder. I set my feet, bent my knees, and pulled. I landed on my back.

When I sat up, my tears started falling and my throat burned. I opened my mouth to yell, but no sound came out.

Stupidly I checked to see if her heart was still beating. It wasn't—I could see it through her broken rib cage.

"Grandad!"

"Coming, boy!"

And then he was kneeling next to me, knees popping and cracking.

"Look what happened to her, Grandad." Her eyes were glazed, cheeks smeared with blood, tongue hanging out. I reached out and touched her neck. "Oh, Snow."

11

I wanted to run home and tell everyone Snow was dead. Our Snow, who gave the most beautiful white fiber every year, our most faithful and dependable packer, whose crias were sold for thousands of dollars, our champion dam. Dead.

Elmo! What about Elmo?

"Grandad! The cria! Where's the cria?" I stood up and looked wildly around.

Grandad cleared his throat. "JT, the dam was probably protecting him."

"We have to check, at least! Find out if he's—" I started crying again.

Grandad waited a minute before he stood up. "That's the way it goes sometimes."

"Well, I'm going to get the FourTrax and look for him." I squeezed my fists, my fingernails making crescent moon shapes on my palms.

"Let's get the fence done, now."

I stared. "Now?"

"JT, you do what needs to be done." He sighed. "It'll help the whole ranch to repair the fence. There's nothing we can do for Snow."

I wiped my eyes and rubbed my fist on my pants. "What about Elmo? I might find him in time to—to—"

"JT, the fence has to get fixed. You think that was the only hungry bear in these parts? Let's suppose another one finds this fence all run through. The guards and packers are still out."

I nodded. I didn't have to hear what would happen to the rest of our herd if the fence wasn't patched soon. "But what about Elmo?"

"We can always hope."

Snow's body was torn apart—there was hardly any skin left on her. Whoever had done this hadn't even eaten her—just killed her. It made me so angry I wanted to kill every bear on the mountain.

"I can't manage it without you, JT." Grandad placed his walking stick and carefully took a step.

We headed toward the fence, Grandad walking silently next to me, letting me cry until I was all cried out.

When we got to the hole, he handed me the wire clippers. "Snip six-foot sections," he instructed. He unrolled the wire and I snipped every six feet, mashing the wire cutters together, squeezing as hard as I could. When we had enough, he showed me how to use the pliers to twist the patch wire onto the old and string it across the gap, tighten it down, and twist it on good and tight.

It was slow, tedious work. I kept turning around and looking at the road, glancing up the hillside. It felt like something big and ugly was going to sneak up behind me any minute. When I remembered Snow lying there all bloody and broken, I felt like my heart had a hole ripped in it.

We wove wire over and under, over and under. Twist the end on, weave, pull, weave, pull, twist, cut. I concentrated on my hands. Over and under, over and under, making a patch as strong as the original fence.

"I should have left them in the barn," I said.

Grandad didn't look up, just kept weaving and cutting. I thought he didn't hear me. Finally, he turned his chin toward me. "The bear is just being a bear, you know."

I snorted. "Sorry excuse."

"It isn't an excuse. It's the truth. The bear only knows to do what a bear can do. Same for the llama." He turned to look at me, right in the eyes. "Same for people."

"I don't get it."

"Someday you will, JT."

The sun was already setting as we walked back. Although the spool was empty, my arms felt ready to drop right off. When we passed the spot where Snow's carcass lay, I wanted to check on it. Grandad put his hand on my arm.

"You won't find anything different, JT."

"I just wanted to see if maybe Elmo's with her."

"The cria? Not likely. Llamas spook at the smell of blood."

The shadows grew longer and Grandad moved slower until finally we saw the lights of the shop and we were home.

12

Greg and Mom were in the shop when I put away the tools. Their boots and jeans were covered with mud, and they slumped on bales of hay, drinking coffee from thermos lids.

"Fix the fence?" Greg asked. "Find any more holes?"

"Snow's dead," I said.

Mom got up. "Oh, honey." She walked over and hugged me.

"Bear got her." I rubbed my eyes but they stung and filled with tears all over again.

"Did you have to put her down?"

"She was already dead."

"Sorry, buddy," Greg said. "The cria, too?"

"We didn't find anything. The bear probably took him first."

Mom nodded. "Probably."

"Unless she was protecting him," Greg said.

I looked up, hopeful. Mom was nodding, not really listening. I sighed. "Did you find them all?"

"Nine bachelors and fourteen yearlings. Dad's still out looking before it gets completely dark. The farther from town they go . . ." Mom's voice trailed off as she took another sip from her cup.

"I'd like to go look for Elmo," I said. "I could use the FourTrax."

"We need to bring in the packers and go get the guards and sheep," Greg said. "Dad hasn't had a chance to do it."

"Then can I go look for Elmo? After that?"

"First, help Greg bring the other herds in. I'll stay with Turre and start dinner."

Greg stood up and stretched.

Mom stepped out, then came back in. "Greg, get that carcass to the burn pit. We don't need it attracting any more critters. And take your rifle with you."

⋇⊱

Greg hitched the flat trailer to the FourTrax. He drove while I held his .22 across my lap. It had been a gift from Grandad and Dad when Greg turned twelve. He let me shoot it when he was in a good mood.

I didn't even ask about the rest of the herd. Snow was dead. I didn't care about anything else.

Greg told me anyway. "Tex is missing with about three dozen bachelors, and Oliver and the yearling herd are gone, too—eighteen or nineteen. Bessie and Lolly lost their crias, but they're okay, and the inside fencing looks like a tank rolled through, knocked down left and right."

Mom had filled the empty stalls in the big barn with stray bachelors and yearlings, where they would have to stay until the fence was fixed. Mixing the herds together and cramming them in with the sires was sure to make them tense. Llamas didn't like to be cooped up for long and they hated to be separated from their herds. Any Kinnaman knew that. "Are we putting the packers in with the sires? What about the sheep and guards? They'll go crazy all together."

"We fix the fences as fast as we can, then turn them out, hopefully before they start fighting," Greg said. "The sires are already raising a ruckus. I had to cross-tie them."

We stopped and loaded Snow's body onto the trailer. I couldn't keep from staring at it as we drove. If I had just left them in the stall . . .

We reached the guards as dark set in. I shook the leads, calling, "Come, llamas, come on."

"Hush," said Greg. "They're already freaked out. Come, llamas, come on. Come, llamas."

The nine guards were huddled together, rears in protecting the sheep, heads out, necks up as they watched us.

High alert stance, Grandad called it. They stood perfectly still, no chewing, no humming, just watching and listening for more trouble. They were two seconds from a blind stampede.

I walked slowly around the herd, not wanting to startle them.

"Where's Sentry?" Greg asked softly. Neither one of us could see the red llama. "Come on, Sentry," I called. Then I heard a soft snort. I dug in my pocket and offered him a biscuit, walking slowly to him. Then I haltered him and led him to the FourTrax.

"Come, llamas," Greg called. "Come on." He started the engine and I climbed on, playing out the lead rope so Sentry could walk behind the FourTrax without breathing the exhaust.

Sentry took a ginger step as Greg gently popped the clutch and moved forward. "Come, llamas," he called.

But they balked. They smelled the blood on Snow's body. They were too skittish, too scared. Sentry wouldn't follow.

Greg put the engine in neutral and took the rope from me. "I guess I'll walk them in," he said. He stood near Sentry's head, petting his neck, talking softly to him.

"I can ride him," I said. "You go get the packers. Sentry, cush."

Sentry swayed and sidestepped and finally settled onto his knees and lay down. I stepped over his shoulder and sat. "Stand."

Sentry stood and started walking. Then abruptly he stopped. "Let's go," I said. I nudged him in the ribs.

He sat on his haunches like a dog and would not get up. Not for a biscuit, nor for anything. I nudged him again. He hummed a low, angry hum.

Was it only yesterday Nicky and I were taking turns on him? It seemed like a long time ago. Everything was different now.

I stood up. "That won't work, I guess."

"Nope," Greg said. "Get behind them and watch in case one of them tries to cut and run."

I shook my head. "I'll go get the packers," I said. "Blue will lead off the FourTrax."

"You'd better wait for me," Greg said. "I'll walk them in, then come back for the sheep."

"We don't have time to wait for that. It's already dark. Let me try."

Greg glanced at the base of the mountain. "Okay," he said. "But get rid of that carcass first, or even Blue won't follow you."

"You better take the rifle." I handed the gun to Greg and he put it over his shoulder.

I drove behind the barn to the burn pit. I pushed and pulled on Snow's body until it finally tipped and slid into the pit, landing on the charcoal and ashes with a soft thump. I rubbed my face into the crook of my arm and went back to work.

In the next field, the llamas were huddled in a tight ring, just as Sentry's herd had been. "Blue," I called, digging in my pocket for a biscuit. "Come, llamas. Come on."

Blue walked, sidestepping and flinching, up to the FourTrax, craning her neck for the treat. I clipped the lead on her halter and pulled. She dragged her feet. She didn't want to obey me. But I put the engine in gear and held on, fighting for each step. She sat down. I tied the lead to the cargo rack with a double half-hitch and started again. "Come on, llama," I said, gritting my teeth. I pulled her off her feet, knowing I wasn't treating her gently, knowing I wasn't treating her with love, the way Grandad did. If only I could call them like he did, just sing to them and they would listen. "Come on, you stupid llama."

Yanked to a standing position, Blue seemed to forfeit. Her head down, she plodded slowly behind me, the fight gone out of her. The rest of the herd followed readily, and I started off before they could spook. I opened the corral gate and she walked in with her neck low and ears flat. She'd given up.

I was ashamed. No Kinnaman had ever treated a llama like that.

In the barn, Buck and Tumtum were kicking and crashing against the boards, humming and orgling— making that bugling sound that llamas make. They got even louder when I brought in the packers. I had to double them up in the stalls with the young ones, stuffing a total of thirty-nine llamas in together. No Elmo. Snow was dead and probably Elmo was, too.

I filled and hung hay nets and then filled water buckets. The full moon was shining through the barn windows onto their backs as the upset llamas stomped and kicked the walls.

When I was done, Greg came in with Sentry's herd. The guards walked hunched and huddled together. He put them in the corral, and we started leading the llamas into the big barn two at a time. Back and forth I walked, my legs feeling like lead sticks. After a while I could only take one llama at a time.

When we were putting up the last of the guards, Dad rode in with five bachelors in tow. He stopped and gave them to me. "Fourteen. I think that's the best we can hope for." He had dark circles under his eyes and his forehead was covered with sweat and grime.

I took the lead ropes. "I'll take them in and bed them down, Dad. There's room in the small barn. Hopefully the dams won't mind these guys too much."

"They don't have a choice tonight."

"A bear got Snow."

Dad glanced at me. "Ah. That's too bad. Where at?"

I told him where we'd found her.

"That's quite a distance from the field. Must have dragged her a bit," Dad said.

I nodded, looking at the ground. I felt sick to my stomach all over again.

"Well. What's done is done," Dad said.

"Seems odd that a bear would come right through the fences like that," Greg said.

"Yeah, that worries me."

My throat felt tight and hot again. "I should have left them in the barn."

Dad bent down and looked at me, then squeezed me tight. "There's no way any of us could have known."

I swiped at my eyes. "Do you think there's a chance the cria made it?"

"We can hope." Dad sighed, his shoulders dropping. "Get the rest of them in, boys."

I put Jordy in with Dusty. The barn was crammed full—two dams in each stall, males separated so they wouldn't spit at or bite each other. I even had to put two yearlings in Snow's stall, where I'd cared for her and Elmo just that morning. The air was filled with warm musky llama smells, stomping and humming—an orchestra of wild music.

I leaned my head against the wall. Fatigue yanked on my muscles, pulling everything down. I couldn't even make my lips stay together. The baseball game seemed like it was ages ago, or like it had been someone else playing. I dragged the lead ropes to the tack room and stared at the hooks, trying to gather the energy to lift my arms and hang them up. Even my eyeballs hurt.

Then I heard a noise—*pop*.

It had to be a gunshot. Greg.

I heard four more quick shots.

I ran over and opened the barn door. A rush of hooves and bodies came toward me. I ducked back as the sheep stampeded into the aisles. The wild music built in wave after wave as bedded llamas got up, swaying their necks and stomping, craning to see or hear or smell what the danger was.

I grabbed a lead rope, slung it over the nearest sheep's neck, and put it in an empty stall. Then the next. Offended bachelors kicked and hummed, irritated by the sheep.

Greg came running in behind them. "Did you get them?"

"Yeah. Did you shoot the bear?"

"Not with a twenty-two," Greg said. "I was scaring off a wolf pack."

"Were they coming after you?"

"I could see their green eyes just behind me."

Together we fed and watered. Greg lit the burn pile and we stood watching the flames swirl around Snow's body. With the smell of burning meat in my nostrils, I trudged back to the house, and the night that had seemed like it would never end finally did.

13

Sunday morning we sat around the table counting up the losses. Tex and Dave and twenty-two bachelors, Snow, eighteen yearlings, and three crias were still missing. Including Elmo. Thinking of him made my stomach hurt.

Dad counted and added on a calculator, staring at the screen as though the number would tell him whether we were in trouble or not. We all knew we were. At Kinnaman Ranch, each llama mattered, and we'd lost almost half of them.

Dad put his pencil down and put his thumbs on his eyes.

"We'll make it," Grandad said grimly.

"Pop, minus the cash those bachelors would have brought in, then the loss to the breeding stock—"

"Could have been worse." Grandad set his fork across his empty plate, tines down. "And we'll keep on keeping on. We didn't lose any packers."

He talked that way, but I saw the tears in his eyes last night when he left the barn.

"But operating expenses, Pop. We needed to sell the bachelors this fall."

"We might sell some packers, then."

"But that'll create a loss in rental *and* in fiber," Dad said.

"We can clip them a little closer this year, boys, and breed all our females in the fall," Grandad answered. "There's still hope."

"Robert, were you going to shave before church?" Mom said.

"God doesn't care about whiskers, dear."

It seemed like there was nothing left to say.

We put on our tying shoes and scuffed out to the crummy. Grandad stood for a moment, looking over the mountains of Chugiak Range. Greg didn't even push me as we climbed in the back of the old pickup. I stared out the window as we drove down Main Street to the schoolhouse.

In the summertime, we met in the birch grove or by the waterfall on Sundays, but for cold or muddy weather we always met at the school. The desks were pushed to the wall, benches arranged, and the school became the church.

As we sang praises, I looked at Grandad. One hand was on his new walking stick and the other was lifted up. His eyes were closed and he was smiling as he sang. I thought, How can you be happy? How can you be sure everything will be okay?

To me, nothing was okay. It was like a hurricane went through our property. My cria was gone. Nothing felt safe.

Pastor Harley stood up. Harley wasn't his real name—it was his nickname because he rode a Harley hog in the summertime. I liked Pastor Harley, but it was hard to listen to him that day. Every time I closed my eyes I saw Snow's bloody carcass or the smoldering fire pit. My herd was gone. I felt like Kinnaman Ranch was ruined.

It must have showed. Nicky came up to me after church and said, "Hey, JT, no big thing, yesterday's game. You'll knock 'em dead next time."

"Our llamas got out yesterday," I said in a zombie voice. "Snow got killed." I didn't mean to talk in a zombie voice. It just came out that way.

Nicky shoved his hands in his pockets. "Sorry, man. That sucks."

I looked at the floor. "Yeah."

"Is your baby okay?"

I shook my head. "We haven't found him."

"Man. You want some help looking for him?"

I looked up. "He was probably bear lunch. Probably the first to go."

"We could just look."

During fellowship time, Grandad and Dad were recruiting help to fix the fence. Grandad stood with his group of sourdoughs, the old-timers discussing how many men and how much wire we needed.

Gabby, Grandad's best buddy, was standing beside him. He asked Grandad what he was going to do about his messed-up ranching. Grandad's eyes twinkled and he opened his mouth to answer but had a coughing fit instead. Gabby pounded his back. "Hey now, easy now," Gabby said. "Are you doing all right these days, Turre?"

Grandad said, "Sure, sure, I'm fine."

Gabby eyed Grandad for a second, then said, "I'm telling you, friend, it's not too late to take up trapping. I've made a fine living." He scratched under his beaver skin hat and this time Grandad laughed without coughing.

"But there's nothing in the world like llamas," Grandad said.

Mom sat sipping tea with Fireweed's women, dressed in clean flannel shirts and dark jeans in honor of the Lord's day. "And if the fiber auction is low again this year . . ." She stopped when I walked up.

"Excuse me. Can Nicky come over after lunch?"

Nicky's mother nodded, then Mom nodded.

"Bring your binoculars," I whispered to Nicky. "We'll go up to the tree house and look around from there."

Nicky made a face. "I don't know if I want to climb up in that old thing."

"Don't be a sissy, Nick. We can see the whole valley from the tree house. Come right after lunch."

I saw my teacher, Miss Julia, standing on the other side of the room. She wore a flower-print dress and a crocheted shawl. Her hair was bundled up on her head. She didn't look like Mom or the other Fireweed women, but that was because she wasn't one; she was from Outside. She was leaving at the end of the school year, like most teachers did. Interior Alaska was too far from her roots, she said. I guessed it took a certain kind of mettle to adapt to the weather. In school Miss Julia showed us slides of huge glittering places like New York and Disney World, Washington, D.C., and Los Angeles, where she went to college. There never seemed to be many trees in those places, and I wondered: if a tree can't put down roots, how can a person?

I slicked down my hair on top as she approached. "Hey, Miss Julia," I said. "We've got trouble on the ranch." I told her about the fences and Snow and my cria, and I got through all of it without sounding upset. "I won't be at school tomorrow. Maybe Tuesday."

"I'm sorry to hear that, Joseph. I'll send your homework. You must stay caught up."

"Yes, ma'am."

Before Nicky left, he said, "Be ready in two hours."

"I'll be ready."

A north wind had carried off the stench from the burn pile. Leaves whispered in the trees. With the sun fully up, Kinnaman Ranch looked hopeful again.

Greg made a salad, Grandad mashed potatoes, Dad and Mom barbecued a chicken, and I started on my specialty—Wild Blue Stir-Crazy Cobbler.

Patches of wild blueberry bushes grew high up in the mountains around Fireweed. Early August, when the summer cooled off and the days got short, was the time to go picking. We had a secret patch, as did every family in Fireweed. Grandad and I'd spent days there the past summer. Wild blueberries were like gold. We bagged and froze gallons of them to use throughout the year. We traded them with our neighbors for eggs or caribou sausage or moose venison. Sometimes we sold the excess to the grocery store. But mostly we made syrup and jam with them, and we ate them in pancakes, waffles, pie, and especially in cobbler.

I'd learned the recipe the past Christmas. Heavy snow had fallen for a week straight, the power went out on the third day, and there were only a few hours of daylight. Once a day Dad took the snowmobile out to the fields to break the ice on the water troughs and set out hay. The temperature got so low, you could burn your hand just touching the outer doorknob. The rest of us stayed inside and we were getting stir-crazy from being cooped up in the house. After Greg and I got in trouble for playing football in the kitchen, Grandad said, "JT, let's have a cooking lesson. Your grandmother always said this was the best recipe for getting rid of the stir-crazies. I better pass it on before I forget it and you two get skinned."

This afternoon I made it just like Grandad taught me. I scooped berries and sugar into a pot and started it cooking. When it was all bubbling and thick, I poured it into a pan. Then I mixed up the cobbler dough—butter, flour, sugar, and milk—and stirred like crazy. I scooped up spoonfuls of dough and carefully placed them on the hot berries. As I worked, a gray cloud settled over Big Sister, hiding the peak and tree line where our secret patch was. A soft mountain drizzle started. Even if I couldn't see the mountain anymore, I could picture in my mind where I wanted to search first.

I put the cobbler in the oven and as the smell of baking blueberries wafted through the kitchen, I mapped out a search route. If Elmo was alive out there, Nicky and I would find him.

14

I folded my map and stuffed it into my backpack along with my survival kit and canteen. Drizzle coated the valley and Kinnaman Ranch.

"Going fishing?" Grandad asked, pointing at my pack.

"Uh—hiking," I said. He wouldn't like for me to be on the mountain with the wild animals stirred up. But I knew to be careful. I just had to search for Elmo.

"I loved to fish as a boy," Grandad said, sitting back and settling his hands in a way that meant he was warming up for a story. "Used to take my pole to school and stop off at the bridge on my way home."

"Sunfish, right?"

"Right. I'd miss chores sometimes, but Mama forgave me when I brought a little supper in with me." Grandad rubbed the top of his head and coughed a huge wheezing cough.

I peered at him. "You okay?"

"Sure . . . sure." He sounded like he had something caught in his throat.

"You keep saying that," I muttered.

His face turned red as he coughed again, and tears and saliva started dripping.

"Pop?" Dad came in. "Put your arms over your head."

Grandad's eyes rolled toward Dad, but his arms didn't move. Garbled noises came from his mouth.

Before I could move, Dad picked up Grandad's wrists and lifted his arms up. Grandad gave a huge wet cough and I reached for a washcloth. I caught his spittle, then brought him a glass of water. "Want a drink?"

Grandad took a tiny sip, then whispered, "I believe I'm on the other side of that one, boys."

"Why don't you lie down for a bit?" Dad asked.

"Sure, sure." This time, at least, the words didn't sound quite so strangled. "Fine idea." Grandad put his walking stick in front of him and leaned.

Dad lifted him out of the chair, one strong arm around Grandad's skinny waist. "Long day yesterday, Pop," Dad said, moving slowly toward the hallway.

"I believe it was," Grandad agreed.

Nicky pounded on the kitchen door, then opened it a crack. "JT! Let's go!"

I watched them move down the hall, step by step, and turn into my bedroom. I could still hear Grandad coughing and trying to catch his breath.

"JT! Are we going or what?" Nicky waved.

I looked down the hall one more time, then grabbed my bag and ran out the door. Nicky loaded our packs onto the cargo rack of the FourTrax. He put his Red Sox cap on backward. "Ready."

I showed him my map. "To the tree house first. We'll do a survey from there. See if we find any clues or any-thing, then search in fifty-yard sections."

"What kind of clues? Body parts? Fur?"

I swallowed. "Yeah. Trampled bushes. Mashed ferns." I hoped I'd see Elmo standing under a pine tree, look-ing lost.

"Then what?"

"That depends on what we find, doesn't it?"

We didn't talk as I drove along the perimeter, up Little Sister Mountain and over to the second ridge. The drizzle made the trail slick, and the FourTrax kept spinning out in the mud. I turned at the salmonberry bush and up the trail to the tree house. When we got there, I climbed the ladder and pushed on the trap-door. It resisted, then moved, hinges screeching in protest. I threw my pack onto the floor, then reached for Nicky's pack.

The mist made a thin, cold fog all around us. I opened my survival kit and took out my rain poncho.

I put the binoculars to my eyes and leaned on the rail. All around Fireweed, bonfires glowed in burn barrels, meant to deflect any rampaging wildlife. A precaution. Trees and undergrowth came into focus. "I'm searching the north side first. You start on the southeast." Nicky put his binoculars to his eyes. "What happened, anyway?"

"A bear broke through the west fence." I pointed. "Either he took them or they got out and got killed."

"Yikes."

"Yeah." Away from the perimeter path I could see the moose trail that led along Wolverine Creek between Big Sister and Little Sister. The drizzle covered the lenses and I wiped them dry on my sweatshirt. "He's black," I told Nicky. "With a white star on his head."

"I remember."

"Okay." We scanned back and forth. My hands got numb in the cold and my neck cramped up. Then my feet fell asleep.

"Was he eating grass yet?"

"No. Just milk."

"Bummer. How old was he?"

"Just two weeks."

Nicky put down his binoculars and stuck his hands in his armpits for warmth. "Do you really suppose—?"

"Just look a little longer." Back and forth I looked,

under every bush, every spindly pine or paper birch. Up to the tree line and down again. After a while, the drizzle stopped and the weak afternoon sun shone across Big Sister. I even searched the rocky peak, but I was beginning to lose hope.

I spat over the rail. "What a bear wants with that many llamas is beyond me."

"The bear was probably after one llama," Nicky said. "They're not pigs, after all. But once they were all loose . . . I mean, all the wildlife is hungry. My dad said it was a hard winter."

"That's what everyone says. But how was it worse than any other winter?"

"Don't you listen to Miss Julia? Habitat loss. More people, less territory."

"Whatever," I said.

Nicky took the binoculars and peered through them at the broken brush. "Is that where you found Snow?"

"No—that was west. Over there." I pointed.

"Too bad the little guy's not white," Nicky said. He opened a bag of chips.

"Yeah."

"Want a chip? Your favorite—salt and vinegar."

"No thanks." I kept searching up the mountain, to the tree line, over, down, up. I drew line after line with my eyes on the mountainside.

Then I saw flattened fern fronds about a hundred yards up the mountain.

"There's a patch of mashed brush." Nicky followed my finger as I pointed.

"Too messy to be a bed."

"Probably a feeding spot," I said. I looked again and saw something dark under a patch of ferns "Look."

Nicky grabbed his binoculars. "Can't tell what it is."

"Maybe Elmo." I stood up to get a different angle.

"Could be. Could be a shadow."

I looked again. All I could see was patch of dark—too black to be a shadow, too small to be a moose. "Let's go."

"JT, it could be a black bear. Or a wolverine."

"I doubt it." My heart started pounding. If it really was Elmo, if he was alive, he was starving. Dehydrated. He'd been without milk for way too long. I had to move fast. "I'm going up there. Come on."

Nicky shoved another chip into his mouth. "JT, I don't know if we should."

"We'll be careful. Wide berth and all that." Give grouchy women and wild animals a wide berth, Grandad always said. Stay as far away as you can and still get your job done. I climbed down the ladder and started the FourTrax.

Nicky followed slowly. "I don't like this," he yelled over the sound of the motor. "We ought to go home and get some help."

"We can do it," I said.

"But I don't want to."

"Of course not. It's not your llama." I didn't have time to explain about being responsible for an animal, or about tending to it and protecting it. Nicky didn't even have a pet hamster. Nicky's dad killed animals for a living. "Are you coming or not? I'll come back and get you if you want to watch from here."

It didn't take him long to decide. He hopped on. I drove north about a hundred yards and stopped, so we could split up and walk down on either side of the black thing. If it was a wild animal, this would give it a chance to escape. Only a trapped animal would attack.

Wishing I'd thought to bring Greg's rifle, I picked up a stick. Nicky got one, too.

"You go over forty paces," I pointed. "Then, when I nod, let's go downhill together. First person to see something, yell."

"Don't yell! Whistle."

"Okay. Let's go." We popped fists and Nicky paced off. He looked back at me and gave a thumbs-up.

The fireweed and ferns fluttered in the breeze. Picking through dead limbs and bushes, we started down.

We'd walked about fifty yards when I heard rustling. I looked up—no birds. I looked around for a moose calf or a rabbit. Nothing. I stepped quietly, feeling like Squanto. My steps made no noise at all. I imagined myself in buckskins. I would have made a good Native American.

I motioned for Nicky to come in a few steps. He shook his head and pointed down. The rustling noise was right in front of him.

I angled off toward him, hurrying. Rustling sounds meant something was alive. I started making a lot of noise, hitting my stick on trees and sliding through brush instead of going around it, trying to give a lot of warning. I did not want to meet up with a hungry bear, or anything else with fangs and claws. But I felt like sprinting down the side of the mountain to find out if it was Elmo.

By the time I got to Nicky I was jogging, and I would have blown right past him and on down the mountain, but he put his hand on my chest. "What are you doing?"

"It might be Elmo!"

I tried to push around him, but he blocked me. "And it might be Smoky Bear ready for an afternoon snack," he said. "Did you forget about that?"

I stopped. "I'm making noise," I said, but I knew he was right. I needed to slow down.

"And if Smoky has cubs, we aren't going to be welcome visitors, if you get what I mean." Nicky stepped in front of me. "So we're going to walk slow and make a lot of noise. Wide berth and a fair warning."

I nodded. "Let's get out our bells."

We took bear bells out of our survival kits. Jingling them as we walked should be enough to warn a bear or moose we were coming and give it time to get away.

"Don't go running off like that. Save it for getting to

first base," Nicky said. He shook his bells and sang. "Jingle bells, jingle bells, the bears all run away."

"You'll scare them off just singing." Actually, I was glad he'd stopped me. Who knows what I might have run into? I could almost hear Grandad's voice. "Think about what you're doing *as* you're doing it, not *after.*"

We jingled our way down the hill, pausing occasionally to listen. The rustling stopped. Then I saw it. The back of an animal, curled up under a sword fern. *"Sst!"* I pointed and Nicky looked, nodding. It didn't move.

"Could be a cub hiding while the sow is out foraging," Nicky whispered.

"It would be in its den, wouldn't it?"

"Wolverine?"

"This low on the mountain?"

Blood raced through my veins as I stood watching the animal. I wanted to get a closer view but didn't dare, not until I knew what it was. I clapped. It twitched. My heart pounding again, I felt a hot ball my throat. "He's alive."

"You gotta be sure it's him first."

I clapped again. This time the animal shifted and a two-toed hoof poked out.

"It's him!" I dropped everything and ran to him. I pushed the fern fronds back and saw his little black head and tiny white star.

"Hey, boy," I said. I reached out and stroked his neck. "Hey, Elmo." He was shivering. His eyes stared dully. He didn't lift his head. His tongue lolled out one side of his mouth.

"Give me my canteen," I said.

Nicky brought over my pack. "You're giving him water?"

"I brought milk." I dripped some milk on my finger and put it on Elmo's tongue. His nostrils flared. I did it again and he pulled his tongue in.

I dropped milk onto my finger and put it inside his cheek. He swallowed.

"Look, he's not taking it," Nicky said. "The milk's running down his neck."

I wiped off his fur. "We've got to get him home and warm him up," I said.

"Let's see if he can stand."

"Come on, llama," I said. Elmo moved his ear. "Come on." His front hoof twitched.

Nicky squatted down. "He's too weak to stand."

I bent down and looked at his leg. "Look, Nicky. He's hurt." Poking through the skin of Elmo's back right leg was a jagged white end of a bone.

"Oh man," Nicky said.

"Hand me my pack."

Swallowing the lump in my throat, I unrolled the canvas from my kit and spread it out on the ground. We lifted Elmo onto it. I unfolded the space blanket and wrapped it carefully around him. Then we carried him up the mountain to the FourTrax.

"You drive," I said. I laid Elmo across the cargo rack and tied him gently with the cord. Nicky pointed the FourTrax downhill and I held on to Elmo. His head rolled and banged on the rack. I put my hand under it and bent close to him, humming the wild music and praying it wasn't too late.

15

The house was dark when we pulled up.

"Now what are you going to do?" Nicky asked.

"Warm him up and try to feed him again." I gently lifted Elmo from the rack and carried him to the tack room. I talked softly to him. "It's okay, buddy. It's okay now." I piled some straw in the corner, away from drafts.

Nicky picked up a handful of straw and threw it, piece by piece. "Do you need any help?"

I sat back on my heels. "You've already helped a lot. Thanks."

"Okay, well, I'll get going, then. I still have homework."

"Okay."

I lifted Elmo onto the straw and covered him with a wool pack blanket. He shivered as I petted his neck.

I heard a FourTrax pull into the yard and heard the engine cut off. Probably Nicky coming back, I thought. Footsteps crunched across the gravel and into the barn. "Joey!" Greg called.

"I found him! He's alive! Elmo's alive!" I opened the tack room door. "He must have—" I stopped and looked at Greg. His eyes were red and his face was blotchy. "Greg? Are you crying?"

"Grandad's at the clinic, Joey."

"Why?"

"He got real sick. They think he had a stroke."

"How bad is it?"

"It's bad. We need to get over there. Now."

I looked at Elmo, then back at Greg. "But he said he was fine."

"Well, he isn't. Let's go."

"No!" I said. Everything was happening too fast. "I need to find a bottle and warm up some milk. He's near starved. And his leg is broken."

Greg put his hands on my shoulders. "Joey. Grandad needs you. Mom and Dad told me to find you and get over to the clinic."

"You do the work that needs to be done," I said stubbornly. "I'll come when I finish tending to Elmo." I unwrapped the canvas and lifted the space blanket. Elmo's ear flicked just slightly. He was too hurt to notice what was going on.

"Oh, that poor thing," Greg said.

"He'll be all right," I said, my throat closing up. My voice came out sounding choked. "He'll be fine."

"He's in bad shape, buddy."

"I'm going to get him some milk."

"Cow's milk?"

"Yeah. What other kind of milk do we have?" I was getting irritated with his questions.

"You can't give him cow's milk. He can't digest it. He needs llama milk."

"Well, how on earth do I get that? Snow's dead, remember?"

Greg sighed. "Joey, he isn't going to make it. Even if you could get another dam to adopt him, he can't stand up to nurse."

"I'll figure something out."

"We need to go," Greg said gently.

"You go. I want to settle him in."

Greg looked at me. "Don't you want to check on Grandad?"

I watched Elmo breathing, his side moving up and down, up and down. In my mind I could see Grandad coughing and turning red, stumbling and falling. Finally I said, "I'll come as soon as I get Elmo settled. He needs me. Grandad's being taken care of, right?"

"Okay. I'll try to explain to Mom and Dad." Greg

scratched Elmo's star. "He's a tough little guy to last out there this long."

I nodded.

"You need anything?"

I shook my head.

"Let him rest. If he makes it through the night, maybe we can try to adopt him out."

"Dad ought to know how to do that. I'll ask him when I get there."

"Dad is busy. Grandad's really sick." Greg's voice broke. "Don't you get it?"

I turned away from him and listened to his footsteps fade away. I petted Elmo's neck and shoulder. His shivering continued, his little hooves shaking against the straw. I wondered what Grandad would do if he had an orphaned cria and no milk. I hadn't known cow's milk would hurt Elmo. I'd thought it was better than nothing. I stuck my finger in his mouth and he feebly sucked it. He could drink, I was sure, if I could find something to feed him. I needed llama milk.

Then I had an idea. I found a widemouthed jar on the shelf. I washed it, then went up and down the aisles looking for the right dam. I stopped at Bessie's stall. She stood in the corner, her head hanging down on its long neck, her muzzle near the floor. "Hey, llama," I sang. "Hey, girl." She turned to look at me, then looked at the wall again. I stepped in the stall and offered her a biscuit. She wouldn't take it. "You miss your baby, don't you, girl," I said.

I ran my hand along her side, then over her rump, then down her withers. I felt her udder—hot and swollen with milk. I bent over and squeezed the milker. Nothing happened. I squeezed again, and she stepped back, wagging her ears. No Kinnaman had ever tried to milk a llama.

I patted her thigh, then gently squeezed the milker again. This time a tiny stream of blue-white milk shot out.

I held the jar up close and squeezed the milker, this time catching the milk. "Snow's baby needs your milk," I explained. Bessie started to hum. I squeezed and squeezed—slowly the jar filled with warm milk. I squeezed until only drops came out. When I offered her a biscuit again, she took it.

I ran into the house and took one of Mom's dish-washing gloves from under the sink. I poked a hole in the end of the littlest finger and tied off the other four. A llama bottle. I ran back to the tack room and knelt next to Elmo. I poured the milk into the glove and it dripped steadily from the hole. Perfect. "Hey, llama." I eased his head onto my lap and coaxed the milk-filled finger into his mouth. He opened his big black eyes. They were dull, like an old chalkboard. I wiggled the finger against his tongue. "Come on, boy," I urged.

He gave a couple of weak sucks, then swallowed. His ears swiveled forward and he sucked at it again.

"Got a taste of it, did you?"

He sucked steadily, swallowing and stopping to take

big breaths. I stroked his cheek and touched his neck and hummed. I hoped I sounded like Snow.

He drained the glove and his head flopped down; he was exhausted. "You rest," I said, "and I'll bring more later."

I haltered him and tied him close to the floor so he wouldn't try to get up and make his leg even worse.

Inside, I rinsed the glove, cleaned up, combed my hair and put on my tying shoes—the shoes for church, for weddings and square dances and airplane rides to Anchorage. They weren't the shoes for ranching. They weren't even comfortable. And when I had finished everything that needed to be done, I got on the FourTrax and drove to the clinic to see about Grandad.

16

There were a few chairs lining the wall by the fireplace, all empty. I walked past the foyer to the first room in the hall. A nurse with vivid blue eye makeup and red lips was scurrying back and forth. She reminded me of a rainbow trout.

From the door I could see his bed. The man lying there looked old and pale and shriveled and small. He had tubes coming from his nose, from his arm, and from under the sheets. Grandad.

My cousin, Charles the First Grandson, came in, suit jacket flapping. I called him Charles the First Grandson because he acted like he was the family prince. He was old enough to be my dad, but didn't have any kids. He wore a gray suit and a pager. His hair was slicked back like he was from Anchorage, even though he'd been born and raised right here in Fireweed. He clapped a hand on my shoulder. "You all right, Joey?"

"I'm fine. He's sick." I pointed to Grandad.

"Ah, Joey." Charles the First shook his head. "Why don't you go across the street and wait in my office?"

"Wait for what?"

Charles the First opened his mouth. Then he closed it and looked at his watch.

"I want to stay with Grandad. He looks scared."

"He probably doesn't even know what's going on." Charles glanced over at the bed. The nurse adjusted Grandad's tubes and wires. His eyes were barely open and he gasped for breath, like he was surfacing after a deep dive.

"I'm staying here," I said.

Charles leaned over the bed. "Hi, Grandad. How are you?"

Grandad's eyes rolled toward him, his mouth working open and shut.

"Grandad, Joey's going to be here with you." Charles the First Grandson talked very loudly.

"He's not deaf," I said. "It's his heart, not his ears."

Charles the First Grandson gave me a look. "Hang in there, old guy." He clapped Grandad on the shoulder and stood up. "Did you talk to your folks?" he asked me.

"No. Where are they?"

"They went to the airfield. We called all the relatives."

"Oh."

The First Grandson checked his watch. "They won't be back for a while. Last chance on the office. I have pretty cool computer games."

"I'll stay here."

"I'll be back a little later, then." Charles walked out of the room. If I'd had a baseball, I would have beaned him in the back of the head with it.

The doctor swooped in, white coat billowing out, going from one side of the bed to the other. "Can you move your hand, Turre? How about your foot? Try to push on my hand."

I stepped back every time he came my way, and then finally I just sat in a chair and waited for him to finish. Grandad didn't move. Not one bit. The sound of his gasping filled the room. I squeezed my eyes shut and felt tears coming.

✢✢

Some time later, maybe hours, Charles the First's sisters, the Twin Granddaughters, arrived from Vermont and California. They breezed into the clinic wearing flapping clothes and high-heeled boots. I called them the Princesses of the Kinnaman family. They programmed computers for big companies and took their vacations at spas in Denver. I was a measly Little League pitcher who walked a lot of batters.

Uncle Del and Aunt V came in next. They were fatter than I remembered, and Uncle Del looked pasty. Aunt V had red hair this time. They'd moved to Anchorage years ago. I couldn't remember them living at the ranch with us, although I'd been told they did when I was younger.

The Twin Granddaughters sucked on twin mochas like they were baby bottles. They whispered about their father, and about him *breaking down*. Uncle Del had left the room crying and they didn't know what to do. I wished they would just put down their coffee cups and hug Grandad.

Dad came in holding Mom's hand. He looked old, a lot like Grandad but with more hair. Greg followed them, hands stuffed into his pockets.

"Dad?" I stood up. "What's going to happen to him?"

Mom put her hand on the back of my neck. "We just have to wait and see." Everyone was looking at Grandad, watching his chest as he gasped.

I couldn't just stand there staring at him and all those tubes. "I found Elmo. He's alive."

Dad looked at me like I was speaking Swahili.

"Dad. Isn't that great?"

He rubbed the back of his neck, as if he was trying to remember something important. Mom put her hand on his back.

"He took some milk," I said. I wasn't sure he was listening, but what else was I supposed to do? "He drank all of it," I said. "I think he's going to be okay." Didn't anyone see that it was something to be hopeful about? Not a big deal, maybe, but something. "He drank it all. He was pretty hungry."

"Cow's milk, Joey?" Mom asked in a tired voice.

"No, I milked a dam."

Dad's eyes focused on mine. "You what?"

"Yeah." I smiled. "He sucked it down, too. As soon as his leg's healed, he'll be able to—"

"What's wrong with his leg?"

"Uh, it's broken."

Dad rubbed his temples and sighed. "Joey, llamas don't recover from broken legs. Their bones are too fragile. You know that."

"That may be true of adults, Dad. Elmo's just a baby. His bones might heal better than an adult's."

"He should be put down." Dad said it like it was just another chore, like repairing fences or mucking out the barn. "It's a waste of time to nurse him along."

"Dad, please. Just listen." I put my fists on my legs, curling and relaxing them until I could be calm. "It's my job to put him down, since he's my llama, right?"

Dad nodded.

"Then I decide when's the right time."

"Joey—"

"And I'm not putting him down until I'm sure there's no other way."

"Don't let him suffer," Mom said. "You don't want him to just lie there and suffer."

Dad looked at her and I looked at Grandad and for a minute his labored breathing filled the room.

"He'll get better if he's going to get better," I said, backing toward the door. "There's still hope."

"Joey, wait," Mom called, but I was already at the door of the clinic and bursting out into the fresh air.

17

Elmo was sleeping, his little neck curled across his feet. Already he seemed to be breathing more deeply. I put on my boots and grabbed the pitchfork to muck out the stalls in the small barn. I kept having to dodge angry packers and protective dams that didn't appreciate the intrusion. I fed, watered, and cleaned up. Then I went to the big barn, where the bachelors and sires were loudly challenging each other over the stalls. I dumped the grain in the bin, quickly forked up the soiled straw, refilled the water bucket, ducked out, and moved to the next stall. I wheeled out load after load of dirty straw, dumping, filling, and dumping again. It was a huge job. Sweat made dirt and bits of straw stick to my neck and arms.

When that was done, I took the jar to Bessie's stall. She was still hanging her head in the corner. I wondered if llamas could get depressed the way people in Alaska did during the long winters. Grandad would say yes. He always said they mirrored the human heart.

I wiped my forehead and stepped into the stall. "Hey, Bessie, hey, girl." I petted her neck. One ear twitched but she didn't raise her head. I scratched her woolly back, watching the moon rise through the window, peeking out over Little Sister. I stood there for a long time, petting and talking. I gave her a biscuit and she took it between her lips, chewing slowly. "It's a small, good thing to have," I told her. I smoothed the fiber on her back, on her still-pooched-out belly. I scratched down each of her legs.

I wondered if llamas cried. Maybe on the inside.

Finally I milked her, and I was almost sorry to leave her alone. I gave her another biscuit. "I'll be back in the morning, girl," I said as I left. She turned her head to watch me go.

Elmo woke up when I put a drop of milk on his nose. He struggled to stand, but I held his chest down. It's a llama's nature to eat while standing, but I couldn't let him try. I touched the glove finger to his lips.

"Sometimes you have to go against nature," I told

him. He forgot about standing and slurped and swallowed away, sounding like a piglet. As he drank, I looked at his leg. It was a bad break. It looked like he had been hit by the huge paw of a bear, or maybe the bear had actually bitten him. The tiny bone had snapped like a toothpick. The upper leg was swollen and the bone was dry along its rough edge.

If Dad saw it like that, I would have to put Elmo down for sure.

When the milk was gone, Elmo laid his head on the straw again, tired from the effort. I petted his neck and sang the wild music so he didn't miss his mother so much. I wondered if his heart was broken like Bessie's. Maybe he was crying on the inside, too.

I was finishing a bowl of stew by the fire when Greg came home. He kicked off his shoes and sank into the couch. I took another bite, watching the flames lick at the logs.

"How's Grandad?" I finally asked. I picked out a hunk of meat and chewed it.

"Better than when you were there. He's talking some."

"He is? That's great!"

"He's pretty wiped out still. But he asked for you."

I looked at the fire some more.

"Did you put down your cria?"

"Nope. I fed him. He's doing better, too." I glanced at Greg, ready for a you're-such-a-stupid-kid lecture.

But Greg just nodded. "When the time comes, you can use my twenty-two if you want. You don't have to ask or anything."

"If the time comes."

"Yeah. I guess."

"Are Mom and Dad coming home?"

"Not tonight. Lou took them some dinner. The whole clan is here."

"Great." I tipped my nose in the air and put one hand on my hair.

Greg laughed a tired laugh. "Yeah, but at least they came for Grandad. Even Gabby came down from the mountain."

I stood up and took my bowl to the kitchen. "Anyone staying with us?"

"Nope. Lou's."

"I'm going to bed, then."

"Hey." Greg looked at me. "Did you, um, want to bunk in my room tonight?"

I remembered bunking with him when I was really small, before Grandma Rose died. I remembered him counting stars with me until I fell asleep. But I wanted to feel close to Grandad, in my room. "Naw."

"If you change your mind, then . . ."

"Yeah."

I crawled between the cool sheets and settled my head on the pillow. Moonlight fell across Grandad's bedspread in strips. I squeezed my eyes shut but couldn't sleep. When I opened them, there was Grandad's empty bed right in my face. I went to the window and looked at the moon, high above Little Sister now. I followed the craggy silhouette of the mountain range as far as I could with my eyes, then looked up at the huge Alaskan sky—dark as velvet. Grandad loved to look at the stars and tell me how high the heavens were. "Light goes six trillion miles a year and those stars are two hundred *billion* light-years away." I remembered Grandad drawing out all those zeroes in the window condensation once, just for fun. Twenty-three zeroes.

I wondered if Grandad could see the mountains and the moon from his window, or if he was looking out the window at all.

I gathered a pile of things he ought to have in the hospital: his pillow, his slippers, and his old black Bible. I'd take them to him if he didn't come home tomorrow.

Then I reached up on the top shelf of the closet for his green army sleeping bag.

I took it out to the barn, spread it on the tack room floor next to Elmo, and fell asleep to the sound of his breathing.

18

I woke to a scratching sound. I blinked and lifted my head. Elmo had his lips curled back, chewing at the wall. "Elmo! Quit that!" I pulled his head away from the boards. He whiffled me and started sucking my finger. "Hungry? Okay, boy," I said. "Just a minute."

I grabbed a biscuit and took it to Bessie. She hummed when she saw me, and stepped toward me when I slipped into her stall. I fed her the biscuit, then milked her as quickly as I could.

Elmo sucked the milk down so fast that I knew he would be hungry again before long. "I'll bring you some lunch today, boy," I promised.

Mom was fixing breakfast when I came in. Greg must have told her about Elmo because she said, "How's the cria?"

"Hungry."

"I'm just here for a quick shower." She came over and gave me a hug. "How're you doing, honey?"

I hugged her and stepped back. "Okay. Is Grandad coming home today? Greg said he was talking."

Mom sighed. "Grandad's very ill."

"How ill?"

"We're taking it one day at a time."

"But Greg said he was awake and talking."

"Yes, JT, he was. But we really don't know how much time he has left."

I looked at the floor.

Mom tipped my chin up so I could see her face. "You need to think about going to see him today."

"Then he's not coming home today?"

"No. How about after baseball practice?"

"Maybe." I slid my foot back and forth on the floor.

Mom nodded. "Greg's going to feed and get started on the fencing. He could use your help."

It took most of the day to feed and water the llamas and run fencing materials and tools out to Greg, but I was able to feed Elmo two more times. He didn't look any better, but he didn't look worse, either. Greg and I dug holes and set posts along an interior break. Late in the afternoon, I heard a sound like screaming in the big barn. Buck and Tumtum were at it again. Buck had torn loose his cross-tie. I took some water and cement to Greg and told him. "The sires are going nuts, and they're making everyone else crazy, too."

"Bring one of them out before they kill each other," Greg said, holding a post in a hole and pouring cement around it. "Put Tumtum in the corral."

I wiped the sweat from my forehead. "Me?"

"I'm heading in after this cement sets. Just holler if you need help."

I went to the big barn with a halter. Buck was stomping and kicking, pushing against the wall. Tumtum was standing at his door, rhythmically kicking it. He looked to be the calmer of the two. I swallowed, haltered Tumtum, and clipped on the lead. "Come on, Tumtum," I said quietly. I opened the stall door and led him into the aisle. "Let's go." He walked obediently next to me. I breathed out. This wasn't so hard. Then we passed Buck's stall. Buck spat and gave a challenge bark. Tumtum reared and lunged at him, jerking me off balance. I fell hard on my side. All I could see was the hooves of a four-hundred-pound llama by my head. I grabbed for the lead as they bit and barked, crashing against the stall at each other. "Greg!" The sires were chest-butting against the wood door, which wobbled crazily, as though it would break off its post any second. "Greg!"

I rolled away and stood up. Buck's cheek was scratched, and the skin showed pink and red. Where was Greg? I walked around the fighting sires and grabbed the end of the lead. My ribs felt like they were on fire. I gripped the rope with both hands and jerked as hard as I could. Tumtum's neck swung toward me. I jerked again. "Come on," I growled. He spat on me—llama slime ran down my neck and into my collar. He strained toward Buck. I'd taken aim with my boot, ready to kick him in the ribs as hard as I could, when Greg ran in.

"Hey! What are you doing?" Greg took Tumtum by the halter and pulled his head down. He glanced at me. "Are you okay?"

"They're fighting," I said.

"Come on, knothead," Greg said, his voice low and steady. He led Tumtum out to the corral. Tumtum acted just like a dog, obeying calmly, the fight forgotten. Greg latched the gate. *"Never* handle our llamas that way. Got that?"

"What was I supposed to do?" I rubbed my side.

He shook his head, walking away. "You just can't lead them yet, Joey. That's all. I shouldn't have asked."

I ducked my head and walked to the house, scuffing lines in the gravel. In all his years of llama ranching, Grandad had never been spat on. That was a llama's greatest insult. I took a shower, scrubbing off the grime of the barn, and dressed in baseball pants and a T-shirt. I grabbed my Eagles cap and shoved it onto my head. Then I ran back and traded that hat for my Kinnaman

Ranch cap, for Grandad's sake. I put his stuff in my pack and hurried to practice.

❖❖

I dropped my pack in the dugout and ran onto the field.

"Hey, JT!" Nicky ran up to me. "How's the baby?"

"Better," I said.

"My dad's coming to help your dad with the fences tomorrow."

"Cool. Thanks."

"Are you okay, man? You look terrible."

I thought of Grandad with tubes and machines and people all around him. I thought of his empty bed at home, and the trouble with the llamas. It was too much to explain. "I guess so."

"Let's go!" shouted Coach Ben.

The team lined up in the field and stretched. My side ached. In fact, every muscle hurt. We started with drills— batting, running, fielding. Grounders, fly balls, line drives.

"Pitchers, over here!" Coach divided us up and organized a scrimmage.

I ran to the mound, took a ball, and looked at it—it felt like a year since I'd last held one.

Nicky stood up to bat. "Let's go!" he yelled, waving the bat behind his head.

"Let's see it, JT!" yelled Coach. "Bat until you hit! Outfield, look sharp!"

I wound up and threw. It hit the dirt at Nicky's feet.

"What was that?" Nicky threw his arm up in the air like I'd done it just to bug him.

The other pitchers snickered behind me. I heard Bo say *"Oh boy"* under his breath.

I threw again. Over Nicky's head.

"Concentrate," Coach said, crossing his arms over his chest.

"We want a pitcher," chanted the outfielders.

"Not a belly itcher," answered the infielders. I turned around and glared at them.

"Hey, enough," called Coach. They hushed.

I wound up and threw again. Nicky jumped out of the way. "Man!" he said. "Are you doing that on purpose?"

I shook my head, kicking a ditch in the dirt. Coach came out to the mound. "What's up, son?"

"I don't know. I can't do it today, Coach."

He lowered his head. "I heard about your grandpa."

I felt my cheeks flush and my throat tighten up. I nodded. I couldn't talk.

"I'm glad he pulled through last night."

Pulled through? I felt like I was going to fall over.

"You wanna go on home, son?"

I shook my head, taking a deep breath. "I'm going over to see him after practice."

"You wanna take a break?"

"I can do it," I said, squeezing the ball and looking at home plate.

But I couldn't. Five pitches—ball, ball, ball, ball. Ball.

The team was groaning louder with every pitch. Nicky sighed and rolled his eyes. "JT, what's your problem? Your grandpa keep you awake last night snoring too loud?"

Everyone cracked up laughing.

"Settle down," said Coach.

Nicky pounded home plate and cocked his bat.

I felt my eyes burning. I glared at him, wound up, and threw as hard as I could. He didn't even have a chance to jump back. I hit him in the thigh. He dropped to the ground, howling and holding his leg.

"Hey!" Coach yelled. "Kinnaman! Off the field!"

"I'm going," I said. I walked to the dugout, got my gear, and left before anyone could see my wet face.

19

The Kinnaman family lined the hallway of the clinic and crowded the tiny lobby. They nodded or said hey as I walked by. I wondered if Coach was going to call my dad or follow me over here. Maybe kick me off the team.

Oh well. I really didn't care.

I walked into Grandad's room. The Princesses and Uncle Del and Aunt V were leaning on each side of the room, like they were afraid the walls would collapse if they didn't hold them up.

"Hey, Joey," said one Princess. She dipped her head and sipped at her cardboard cup.

"Hi."

Uncle Del put his hand on my shoulder. "Joey."

His eyes were squashed above his poochy cheeks. His beard made him look like a goat.

"Sir?"

"Your granddad's real tired. We're trying to let him rest."

"Oh." I looked down at the floor.

Aunt V said, "Would you like to draw a picture?" She started digging in her purse.

"No. I came to see Grandad."

"Well, I suppose it wouldn't hurt to say hello," said Aunt V.

One of the Princesses grabbed me and her bracelets clanged. She hugged me with cold hands and I almost choked on her lemon-smelling perfume. Then she let go and grabbed a tissue from the box and held it to her nose. The other Princess started rubbing her shoulder.

I thought, Oh brother. I stepped around them, next to Grandad's bed. I moved the tubes and wires very carefully, so they wouldn't pull, and sat on the edge of the bed. I put my hand on Grandad's arm. "Hey."

He opened his blue eyes; they were rimmed with red. They looked like they were floating in water. He shut his mouth and opened it again, trying to get enough air to talk. "JT," he croaked.

"Hey, Grandad." I sang it, like he was a llama. He smiled and patted my hand.

Aunt V gave a silly little sob and walked out, but Grandad didn't look like he'd heard her.

"You have a game?" He blinked slowly; then his eyes settled on my face.

"Practice."

"How was it?" His voice sounded like it was coming from far away.

"Okay, I guess." I covered his hand with mine.

He nodded slowly. His hand was bruised where the needle went in. His mouth hung down at one corner, and a spot of drool glistened there. I wiped it off. I sat on the edge of the bed and looked at him. I tried to smile. "How are you feeling?"

"Hungry."

"Me too." I took his hand and traced the blue veins spiderwebbing under his skin. One by one, the clan left the room until it was just the two of us, Grandad and me, hanging out.

"Something on your mind?"

I wanted to ask if he was going to be okay, but instead I said, "Would you put down a cria with a broken leg?"

"Why?"

I told him about Snow getting killed. He didn't seem to remember. I told him how I'd found Elmo in the woods and about his leg being broken.

"But I'm milking Bessie and he's taking a bottle. He's getting stronger."

"He can't . . . stand up?"

I shook my head. "But he keeps on trying. He wants to."

Grandad swallowed, grimacing on the right side of his face. "There was a day . . . I might have put him down," he said. A huge cough shook his body. I lifted his arms up until it passed. "But if he's keeping on . . . I guess I'd help him if I could."

I hugged him then, as tight as I could without hurting him.

"I brought some stuff for you." I opened my pack and took out his pillow. Gently, I raised his head and put his pillow behind it.

"Ah," he sighed. He looked at the flowered edges and cursive *TK* on the pillowcase. "Your grandmother embroidered this, you know. Fifty-odd years ago."

"Wow."

"I miss that woman." He looked out the window at Big Sister. The sun had turned the hillside greenish gold. "I wonder if she looks like I remember her."

I picked at a thread on the bed. "Probably."

"Probably better."

I nodded.

Grandad swung his eyes back toward me. A tear leaked down his cheek. I brushed it off.

"Won't be long before I find out, JT."

"Grandad." I squeezed his hand.

He leaned back again and looked steadily at me. "Thought you should hear it from me, son."

"Get better and come home," I said. I barely choked it out.

"I'm not afraid and don't you be. Be sad, but don't be afraid of what life brings along."

I held his hand, not knowing what else to do. His veins crisscrossed under the brown spots and wrinkles. Old working hands. "Want me to read to you, Grandad?"

"Sure, sure."

I opened his Bible and read Isaiah 55, about how the heavens are higher than the earth. He whispered the verses as I read them, his lips barely moving.

"Is that your favorite part of the whole Bible?"

"Oh no. My favorite is . . ." He stopped for a long ugly cough. " 'Come to me, all ye who are weary and heavy laden, and I will give you rest.' " He sighed. "I'm going to go, JT. Do you understand?"

Somehow I already knew that, deep inside, but to hear him say it felt like a piece of me breaking off and crashing down a river.

I nodded. Then I closed his Bible and looked at the worn leather cover. I kissed the top of his bald head. "I'd better check on Elmo, Grandad."

"Watch for infection. Llamas are fragile, like people."

"Okay."

"And JT? If the time comes to let him go, then you be big enough to do it, even if you don't want to. Hear?"

"I will."

I walked out past the cousins and aunts and uncles—

all the Kinnaman family from Alaska and Outside, and pushed through the doors, taking great gulps of evening air. I started up the FourTrax and rode away, accelerating and shifting so fast that I could barely hear Dad calling after me.

But I didn't stop.

20

Elmo made it through the night again. I milked Bessie and fed him and then I went to my room, kicked off my boots, and crawled into bed. I stayed there all day, looking at Grandad's side of the room. I didn't want any breakfast, or any lunch. I just lay there, thinking about everything, until it was time to milk Bessie again.

When I opened the door this time, Elmo's ears swiveled toward me and he lifted his head. He nickered like a foal, which made me laugh. "You're not a horse," I told him. "Llamas hum." I hummed, to remind him. I petted his head and scratched between his long delicate ears. He nosed my hand and when I held up the glove, he bit the finger, sucking hungrily.

"Hey, JT."

I looked up. Nicky stood in the doorway. "Miss Julia sent your assignments." He put his books on a bale of straw.

I looked at Elmo again and smoothed the soft fiber on his neck.

"How's he doing?"

"Fine."

"Can I watch you feed him?"

"If you want."

Nicky squatted down next to me on the floor, and we watched Elmo drink his bottle. "Sure is cute."

I jiggled the glove to work the air bubbles out. I couldn't think of anything to say to him.

"Hey, JT, I didn't know." Nicky picked at his shoe. "About your granddad being sick. Sorry."

The rubber glove flattened as Elmo drained the last drop. He swallowed and sucked for more. I pulled the finger out of his mouth. "I shouldn't have beaned you, anyway. I'm sorry, too."

"It's okay," Nicky said happily. "Man, have you got an arm!" He rubbed his thigh. "You ought to see the bruise!"

I smiled. Nicky was quick to forgive, that was for sure.

Elmo pushed with his front feet, trying to get his back

legs under him and stand up. I held his halter until he quit struggling.

Nicky pointed at Elmo's broken leg. "You know, that looks pretty messed up."

"Yeah. It needs a splint or something."

"I helped my dad set our dog's leg after it got caught in a trap."

"You did?"

"Yeah. It wasn't that hard."

I could tell by looking at the jagged white edge that something needed to be done with it soon. "Hey, I have an idea. You go find a good stick. I'll get some rags and soapy water. At least we could clean it up and keep it from getting infected."

Nicky jumped up and ran for the woods. "Be right back," he called over his shoulder.

I sat back with my hands on my thighs. I patted Elmo's back. "Don't worry, buddy. We're going to fix that leg."

I lined up the supplies: leather gloves, water, soap, bandages, and a few other things. Nicky had found a smooth straight stick. "That ought to do it," I said. "Shave the bark off, would you?"

I rolled a towel under Elmo to make his leg more comfortable. "Okay, the first thing we have to do is clean it."

"No kidding. Gross." Nicky made a face.

"Here. Put on these gloves and don't let him kick. Just hold him down. If a llama can't get his head up, he can't stand up at all."

Nicky gently gripped Elmo's front legs and lay across his shoulders. "Ready."

I took a deep breath and opened the bottle of hydrogen peroxide, pouring some on a rag. I dabbed around the wound, circling closer and closer to the torn skin. The peroxide fizzed and bubbled. Elmo closed his eyes.

Then I poured peroxide over the broken bone and jagged skin. Elmo flinched, crying out and kicking weakly, but Nicky held on.

"It's okay, llama," I sang softly. "It'll be okay."

Nicky stroked Elmo's neck. Elmo's eyes were wide open now. I could see whites around the black. I felt just as scared as he looked.

"How'd your dad do it?"

"He just sort of snapped it back in place, I think."

"Did it work?"

"I guess. The dog always limped a little."

"Great." A lame llama can't carry a pack. A lame llama can't be rented out to hikers or be trained as a guard or shown at the state fair. "I hope he heals better than that. I want him to be good as new."

"Well, he just can't get hurt like that and be good as new."

I looked at Nicky.

"But," Nicky said, "he could still turn out pretty good."

"Yeah." I put one hand on either side of the break. My plan was to pull the broken pieces apart, straighten the twisted bone, then push them back together. Somehow I hoped the ends would pop back inside his skin. I dabbed the skin with the rag, loosening the dried blood and gently washing away the dirt.

"Okay. Hang on, Elmo." I took a deep breath. Nicky tightened his grip.

I pulled.

Elmo let out a scream like a rabbit getting its neck broken. He struggled to stand. Nicky rolled off him. I fell backward. Elmo's cries filled the tack room.

"Hey, Elmo, it's okay. Hey llama, hey," I sang, trying to calm him.

"What's going on in here?" The tack room door banged open.

"Mom!"

"Joseph Turre Kinnaman, *what* are you doing?" Mom's eyes were huge.

"Trying to fix his leg." I hung my head as Elmo continued to bawl. I petted his head. All I'd done was hurt him. Maybe Dad was right about putting him down. He was definitely suffering now.

"Oh, honey." Mom pushed her frizz away from her face and let out a long breath. "Oh, honey," she said again. She put one hand against her cheek.

"I don't want to put him down. He keeps on trying to

get better." When I said it out loud, it just sounded like a stupid reason to let him suffer. "He keeps trying, Mom."

She sighed again and rubbed her arms. She looked really tired, like she'd been up all night. "Does Dad know what you're doing?"

I shook my head. "But he said it's my job to take care of Elmo as I see fit. I'm not putting him down. Grandad wouldn't. I won't let you or Dad or anyone else do it, either."

Mom looked at me for a long time; then she looked at Elmo. Nicky stood up and brushed off his legs.

"Greg's home. Let me get him to help us," she finally said.

I wanted to tell her thank you but my throat hurt too bad to talk, so I just hugged her tight.

There was still hope.

21

Mom took charge. I was to be ready with the peroxide and iodine, and Greg would pull. Nicky would hold Elmo's head down and Mom would set the bones.

Mom used the clippers to shave Elmo's leg. I painted the skin with iodine, turning it dark yellow. Then she looked at the bone from underneath and both sides. "Looks like we'll have to pull and twist, this way." She showed Greg. "So the ends will match up." She peered at it awhile longer. "It's not a bad break. I've seen worse."

That sounded like good news. "On a llama?"

"No," Mom said.

"Of all the stupid things," Greg was saying. "When a llama goes lame there's no way it'll ever—"

"I *know,* Greg," I interrupted. "Try to say something helpful."

"You've still got a lot to learn." He shook his head. "Now let's see what we can do for your Elmo."

Nicky held Elmo's head in his lap, petting his black neck.

"Okay," Mom said. "On three, Greg, pull the lower leg toward you, gently. I'll get the upper bone in position, and then we'll set it. Joey, you wash the bone and skin down with peroxide. Keep pouring and stay calm. It's going to get loud in here."

"Ready." Greg braced his legs.

"Ready." My heart was racing and my hands felt cold and wet.

"Ready."

"One. Two. Three."

Greg gripped and pulled. Elmo started screaming again, thrashing with his three good legs. I poured peroxide on his leg. It splashed onto the skin and foamed. My gut twisted as he screeched and bleated and cried. He sounded like the pain might kill him. I felt like it might kill me, too.

Mom pulled and suddenly the bone disappeared inside the skin. She yelled over Elmo's screams, "Twist! A little more! Okay! Back! Stop!" Her fingers ran along the break, feeling the edges through Elmo's skin. "There."

His head thrashed back and forth. Elmo sounded like a person now, a crying baby.

Mom threaded a needle with fishing line and sewed the jagged edges of skin together. Then she stood back. "Joey do you want to finish this?" I took the two ends and tied them with one of Grandad's fishing knots.

"There," Mom said.

Elmo lay on Nicky's lap panting, eyes rolling wildly. It was pitiful.

I soaked the stick with peroxide and gave it to Mom. She laid it against Elmo's leg, tied it tightly with rags, and wrapped the whole thing in cloth bandages. When she tied the last strip on, she said "There" again and sat back. "Now we wait and hope."

Greg wiped his hands on his pants. "Good work, Mom."

Mom was gathering the towels and water. "All that work at the vet's office before I married your dad wasn't for nothing."

"Say, how's Mr. Kinnaman?" Nicky asked.

Mom and Greg looked at each other in a way that meant Nicky and I weren't going to hear the whole truth. "He's breathing better," Mom said. "Joey, do you want to come see him tonight? Or tomorrow?"

"Maybe," I said. "He'd probably like to hear about Elmo's leg."

"Well, I'm going to start my chores," said Greg.

"Me too." Mom gave Elmo a rub on his head. "I'm

headed back to the clinic after that. Greg will be here if you need anything."

When Greg and Mom left, Nicky and I switched places. Elmo lay still, the splint holding his leg out straight. "Looks good," I said.

"Yeah."

I smiled at Nicky. "Thanks for your help and all."

"I'm sure glad your mom showed up." He grinned back. "Could have been ugly."

Elmo let out a big sigh and I petted his cheek, thinking about how much it must have hurt.

The sun glanced through the tack room window, showing bits of dust floating through the air. Nicky said, "Well, hey, JT, I got chores, too." He stood up.

His curly hair was a tangled mess. He had dirt on his face and his shirt had gotten ripped somehow. "Thanks," I said.

"Yeah, no big thing." He patted Elmo before he left, and then my llama and I were alone again.

22

The next morning, I milked Bessie, but when I put the rubber finger in Elmo's mouth, he didn't even try to suck on it. He tried to curl up and sleep, his cast sticking out.

The sounds of men talking and laughing brought me out to the yard. Two dozen of Fireweed's men had turned out to fix our interior fences. They were carrying hammers, wire cutters, buckets of U-shaped nails, rolls of wire. They pushed wheelbarrows and pulled trailers loaded with boards and posts.

Mom came outside and stood on the porch steps. The men hushed and looked up at her.

"I can't tell you what it means to us to have you here helping," she began, gripping one hand with the other. She swallowed and touched the corner of her eye with a knuckle.

"Now, Sadie, it's what neighbors do," said Gabby. "If there's something I can do to aid Turre Kinnaman or his folk, I'm going to do it."

The Fireweed men nodded and murmured.

Greg said, "I'll take you out and show you what needs doing."

"Let's get going, then."

The group moved off like a parade for a builder's supply.

"Joey!" Mom called when she saw me.

"Yes, ma'am?"

"Come inside. I need your help getting lunch."

I glanced back at the tack room before I shut the barn door and went into the house, splashing water on my face. I hoped Elmo would feel better after some more rest. I took two bags of blueberries from the freezer, mixed up a triple batch of Wild Blue Stir-Crazy Cobbler, and put it in the oven.

Then I started peeling potatoes, my least favorite job in the world. I could muck barns all day, but peeling potatoes was a serious bore. Besides that, I always nicked one of my knuckles. The little brown skins landed in the sink, making a small mountain. I made two ridges and pretended it was Little Sister. When I got done piling up Little Sister, I started making a Big Sister.

"Uncle Del called. Grandad's feeling a little better this morning," Mom said as she tore lettuce for salad.

I nodded. I finished the base of Big Sister, trying to aim the peels so the mountain grew evenly.

"He did have a stroke, though."

I nodded again. Big Sister started to tilt to the left, so I started aiming at the right side, trying to even it up again. The peels flew off the potatoes, sticking to the sides of the sink.

"We're just taking it one day at a time," she said again.

I peeled faster and faster. "What's to keep that bear from coming back and tearing up the fence again?"

Mom glanced at me. "The ranger and his team have been tracking him since Saturday. They found dead llamas three miles away. Anyway, when they catch him, they'll dart him and carry him off farther into the Interior. Most bears don't behave that way."

Last year a bear was digging in the school garbage. A ranger shot him with a tranquilizer and flew him to the Brooks Range. Seemed like a lot of hassle for a stupid bear, but nobody wanted to kill it. Alaskans are supposed to be proud of their bears, but I wouldn't mind killing this one. Somehow it seemed like that bear was responsible for a whole lot of trouble at Kinnaman Ranch.

"If I see him, I'm shooting him."

"He was just being a bear, Joey."

"You sound like Grandad," I said. The Big Sister pile developed a huge hole in the side, like a volcano had erupted, ruining it from the inside out. I started peeling faster, covering the Sisters in ash, dropping one slippery white potato into the bowl and grabbing a brown one. I peeled so fast I could barely hear Mom over the *slick slick slick* noise of the peeler.

"Dad'll be coming home soon to get cleaned up and have lunch."

I wondered if Elmo was hungry yet. I wondered if he was still alive, out there aching. I wondered if you could get hurt so bad you just quit breathing. Sometimes it felt like it.

I scooped the peelings into the compost bucket and rinsed the sink. Then I set the potatoes to boil, peeled a pound of carrots, and made a batch of biscuit dough. When the cobbler came out of the oven and the biscuits went in, I asked, "Mind if I check on Elmo real quick? I'll be back in to set the table."

"Joseph Turre"—Mom turned to me—"do you want to go back to the clinic with Dad today and see your grandfather or not?"

"Well." I scooped up a handful of peels and squeezed them. "Elmo needs me."

She nodded. "Go check on him, then. But don't forget your granddad needs you, too."

In the tack room I could see where Elmo had struggled. Straw was scattered across the floor and he was panting like he'd been running.

"Hey, boy," I said. "Hey, Elmo."

His eyes rolled toward me.

Slowly, I stepped forward, trying not to scare him. I stretched out one hand and touched his side. He flinched. I stroked him slowly and gently, humming the wild music.

His tag looked fine, his umbilical cord looked fine. But something was wrong. At first I thought it was just from having my hands in the cold water. I touched his belly, his ears, and his cheek—Elmo was too hot.

"Oh no," I said out loud. I felt him again. He had a fever.

All Kinnaman ranchers knew that llamas rarely came back from a fever—they were just too fragile. I sponged Elmo down with a damp cloth and then I did what I'd seen Grandad do once when Sentry was sick.

I knelt down next to Elmo and prayed.

23

We pulled the picnic table to the yard and laid a slab of plywood across some sawhorses so the men of Fireweed could sit down and eat.

Back and forth I went, from the kitchen to the yard, with platters of stewed chicken, bowls of mashed potatoes, and pitchers of gravy and milk. The men liked my cobbler. It had earned a blue ribbon at the state fair two years in a row, after all, and that was a fact. I filled water glasses and brought second helpings, all the while thinking about Elmo, hot and panting from fever in the tack room. He wouldn't even take a drink.

I climbed onto the counter and scrounged up as

many mugs as I could find, then poured coffee. Mom and I served it. The men said thanks as they brought their plates in. They went back to their own jobs for the afternoon but promised to come again the next morning to finish up. When they left, Mom fixed me a plate and a cup of hot mud and I sat down in the kitchen, but I could barely make the food go down my throat. I drank the mud and put my leftovers in the fridge.

Then I tackled the Denali-size mountain of dishes. Afterward I wanted to sponge Elmo down again, but my plans all changed when Dad walked in the door. His hair was stuck to the sides of his head. His eyes were blood-shot and he shuffled his feet as he walked to the table and sat down.

The first thought I had was *Did it happen?* I jabbed a spoon into the gravy and waited for him to talk.

He slumped in his chair. Mom brought over a cup of coffee. "They got a lot done, Robert."

"Gabby told me the whole northwest corner is re-fenced." Dad took a long drink of coffee and sighed. "He stopped by to see Pop on his way home."

We all waited. If Gabby had stopped to see Grandad, then . . .

"He's taken a turn for the worse," Dad said finally.

I let out my breath—I hadn't realized I'd been hold-ing it.

"They turned up his oxygen, but his fingers are still blue."

Mom leaned over and said something into his ear.

Dad picked up his cup and followed her to the kitchen. They talked quietly so I wouldn't hear them. Mom wiped a tear off her cheek and they hugged.

"Well, one thing at a time," Dad said. "How're the herds doing?"

"Restless."

"They're really loud in the barn," I said. "Greg put Tumtum in the corral, but Buck hasn't quieted down any." My cheeks flushed. I wondered what Dad would think if he knew Tumtum spat on me.

"It won't be but a day or two before we can turn them out again." Mom filled a plate, set it in front of Dad, and rested a hand on his shoulder. "The boys are handling things fine, Robert."

Dad nodded, spearing a piece of chicken.

"Did Mom tell you about Elmo?"

"Who?"

I looked at Mom. "Snow's cria."

Dad shook his head. "I'm sorry, son. It's a tough thing sometimes, ranching animals."

"We set his leg yesterday."

Dad took a bite of chicken, chewed it slowly, then set down his fork. He swallowed and took a sip of coffee. "What for?"

"Because he kept trying to get up." I knew that sounded stupid.

Dad waited. "And?"

"And I didn't want to put him down." I shrugged. "So Mom and Greg helped me set his leg. He's got a splint on."

Dad ate a few bites, really slowly, like he didn't want the food at all. He didn't look mad. He didn't look proud. He didn't look anything.

I took a breath. "And now he has a fever." My head started throbbing and my throat closed up for about the millionth time. "He's really sick."

Mom sighed and sat in a chair.

Dad didn't waste any time. "That's why you should have put him down when you saw his leg was busted. Llamas don't come back from a shock like that."

I ducked my head. I knew he was right. "I just didn't want to."

"Do you want him to suffer?"

I shook my head.

"Well, Joseph, we're going up to see Grandad right after lunch."

"All of us?"

"All of us. And when we get back"—Dad put down his fork and looked at me—"I expect you to do what needs to be done."

"Can't I stay here?"

"We all need to be there just now." Dad's eyes were rimmed with red circles. He looked like he'd been in a blizzard, snow-blind and confused.

I rinsed my plate and sat in the mudroom waiting. I picked up my brown shoes, the ones for special things. Like going to the clinic to see your Grandad.

It was a long time before I could see to tie the laces.

24

The Quonset hut was buzzing. The Princesses were there, as well as Charles the First and all the aunts and uncles. Charles the First was stepping around in a crazy dance, trying to get better reception with his cell phone. Uncle Del had found a spot near the nurses' station where he could check his office e-mail.

Pastor Harley stood next to Gabby, who sat next to Grandad, holding his hand. Pastor Harley whacked me on the back. "Joseph Turre Kinnaman. How are you holding up?"

"Okay." What was I supposed to say?

"How's the llama business treating you?"

"Well, that's what I want to talk to Grandad about."

Gabby put out his cane and Pastor Harley helped him stand up. "I'll check on you later, sourdough," Gabby said, patting Grandad's leg.

I sat next to Grandad's bed. He was lying on his side. His mouth was working like a fish trying to gulp in air.

"Hey, Grandad."

His eyes opened. "JT?"

"Yeah, it's me."

"I've . . . been looking for you."

"We operated on my cria yesterday."

"You . . . what . . . now?" Grandad craned his neck to get a better look at me. I hunched down so I was in front of his face.

"Operated. On Elmo, my cria." I explained about setting Elmo's leg and sewing it up with fishing line. "And I tied it off with your twenty-five-pound Chinook knot," I finished.

Grandad laughed, then coughed a long wet cough. I grabbed a tissue and he spat into it. When he could talk again, he asked, "How'd . . . the cria . . . take it?"

"Uh, well, he's not doing too good just now."

"That so?"

"He's feverish. Spiked up this afternoon."

"Did you . . . ask . . . Robert?"

"Dad said to put him down." I looked at a tar spot on my jeans. I started scratching at it.

Grandad coughed. "But . . . you're not going to . . . eh?"

"No!" I squeezed my eyes shut and saw Elmo's little face, his mouth sucking on the glove finger, those big black eyes blinking at me. "When he's well enough to stand, I can adopt him out to Bessie."

"He worth it?"

"Oh yeah."

Grandad shifted his leg under the covers and picked up his left hand with his right. "Needs antibiotic . . . kill the infection."

Antibiotic—that was expensive medicine that had to be flown in from Outside. Dad only used it on for-sale llamas and the best breeding stock. "Do we have any?"

"Sure, sure." Grandad tipped his head back against the pillow and paused for breath. His voice was whisper soft. "Yellow medicine . . . in the fridge. Three cc's . . . ten pounds."

I repeated that over and over in my head. "Do you think he's worth it?"

"I trust . . . your . . . judgment."

Hope soared in me like an eagle in flight. "Thank you, Grandad!"

He waved his hand toward the nightstand. "How about . . . reading from Isaiah now?"

I moved his tubes and wires and lay down on the edge of his bed, sharing his pillow. I opened his Bible as he closed his eyes. I found the part I was looking for, the part about soaring on wings of eagles, and read until Grandad fell asleep.

I must have fallen asleep, too. When I woke up, it was late. Mom and Dad sat in the corner, holding hands. The nurse with the rainbow makeup came in, unhooked an empty bag, and hooked up a full one on the pole. When she leaned over and felt for the pulse on Grandad's wrist, he woke up and looked at her. She smiled, her bright lips making two red lines across her face.

"Good night . . . what happened to you?" Grandad croaked.

I giggled.

The nurse frowned and looked at her watch. Then she wrote on his chart. She opened a drawer and pulled out what looked like a sponge on a lollipop stick. She swished it in a cup of water and held it to his mouth.

Grandad clamped his lips shut and turned his head away.

"To freshen your mouth," she said.

"No thanks," he said.

"You need your breath freshened."

"You're welcome to it," Grandad said.

I laughed out loud. I couldn't help it.

The nurse said "Humph" and threw the sponge-pop in the trash can.

"Wide berth, eh?" he whispered.

She slapped the clipboard closed. "I'll check on you in a little while, then."

"Can't wait." He winked slowly and I cracked up laughing again.

After she left, the family, Gabby, and Pastor Harley came back. They stood by the bed.

"What's the occasion?" Grandad asked, looking at them one by one.

Mom's eyes filled with tears and she left. Dad followed her.

"Bad one, Grandad," I said.

He shrugged. "Trying to have . . . a little fun." Then he looked at me again. "JT? You give your cria that shot yet?"

"Not yet, Grandad. I'll do it as soon as I get home." I squeezed his hand. Mom and Dad came back in with tissues in their hands.

"Better . . . take care of him," Grandad said. He erupted in a big cough again. "No time to lose."

I stood up and looked at Dad.

"On a llama ranch," Grandad said, "life keeps on keeping on." His voice was scraggly.

Dad nodded, looking at me.

I leaned over and hugged Grandad. "I love you, Grandad," I said.

"Love you too, JT."

25

Elmo's head lolled sideways, his huge eyes half open. He was burning up with fever. I opened the tack room door and set up a fan to blow on him. I wiped a wet rag on his ears and his downy neck. There wasn't much time.

The antibiotic wasn't on the shelf in the refrigerator. It wasn't in the freezer. I didn't see *any* bottle of medicine, yellow or otherwise.

I searched the shelves in the tack room until I was sneezing and covered with dust. Then I went to the shop. The old metal refrigerator hummed in the corner.

The bottom shelf had bottles of vaccines for the crias, and the top shelf had iodine and worming paste. I tried to remember what Grandad had said. Shelf *in* the fridge? Shelf *above* the fridge? *Which* refrigerator?

I ran into the house and shoved my arm into the back of the freezer. I felt a small glass bottle. Wrapping my fingers around it, I brought it out. This was it—the antibiotic that would save Elmo.

There was no time to weigh him. I warmed the bottle in my armpit, thawing the medicine. I took the needle from the box and filled the syringe with five cc's, hoping he hadn't lost much weight while he was in the woods.

Then I took a deep breath. "Here goes," I said out loud.

Elmo lay flat on the straw, not moving. I squatted next to him. His ribs hardly moved as he took shallow breaths.

I gently pressed his thigh, searching for the thickest part of the muscle. I took the cap off the needle, tapping the side of the syringe to release the air bubbles.

I held his leg, although he was too weak to move. I swabbed the skin with alcohol, then poked the needle into his leg muscle and pushed the medicine in. I let out my breath. Rubbing the medicine into his muscle, I whispered, "Okay, boy. Now we wait."

I milked Bessie, but even though I tried and tried to get Elmo to take it, he just wasn't strong enough to drink.

I spread out my sleeping bag and lay next to him,

listening to him pant. I was afraid he was almost dead. After a short prayer, I fell asleep with my arm on his neck.

I woke up to a cleat nudging me in the side. "Get up!"

I poked my head out of my sleeping bag and opened my eyes.

"Practice in fifteen minutes! We gotta go!" Nicky nudged me again.

I sat up, searching for Elmo. He was curled up near my feet. I felt his ears and sighed. His tongue hung out and his gums were dry. His fever hadn't changed.

"Boy," Nicky said softly, squatting down. "He doesn't look so good anymore, does he?"

I shook my head. I couldn't talk. I'd thought Elmo would be fine after he got the antibiotic.

"Are you coming to practice?"

I shrugged. "Coach probably isn't going to play me anyway."

"He has to!"

I looked up. "He does?"

Nicky clapped my shoulder. "Bo broke his arm."

"Get out."

"Really. He fell out of a tree at recess. You *have* to pitch." Nicky stroked Elmo's neck. "If you want to. It's no big thing if you don't. Everyone would understand."

Me? I couldn't believe it. Everyone had hated me at

the last practice. Head pitcher? Still, I knew I was good enough to do it. I might walk a few. But I could always strike out the next one.

I looked at Elmo again. There might not be much hope for him. But if there was anything I could do to help him, I would do it. "Let me see if he'll take some milk, and give him another dose of antibiotic. Tell Coach I'll be a few minutes late for practice."

"He'll make you run the field if you're late."

"Then I'll run."

Nicky dropped his glove and bat. "And I'll run with you."

I grinned. Nicky was a real buddy.

We milked Bessie and together we were able to hold Elmo's mouth open and coax some milk down his throat. Most of it ran down his neck, but I was sure some got to his stomach. Then we unwrapped his leg and checked his stitches. Deep purple bruises covered the skin around the break. His leg was hot and swollen, but the fishing line was holding.

I gave him another shot, then rushed inside to change.

We had to run the field three times. I groaned, but it actually felt good to stretch my cramped muscles.

Coach said, "JT, we're short a pitcher."

Nicky grinned.

My heart jumped in my chest. "Yes, sir."

"You think you can put in a little extra practice?"

"Sure."

He looked down at me. "Are you sure you're sure?"

"Yeah, I guess," I said.

He nodded. "Okay then. Get on the mound and we'll see where you're at."

Allan suited up to catch. I threw a few slow ones. My shoulder was loose and relaxed.

Bo came out to the mound, his arm in a blue cast. I swallowed and said, "Sorry about your arm, Bo."

"Thanks."

"Hey." I kicked the dirt. "If you have any advice for me, I'll hear it."

Bo looked at me and nodded once. "Point your toe. Keep your whole body behind the ball on your follow-through and you'll get more speed," he said.

"Thanks." I threw. The ball smacked the leather.

Bo whistled. "Nice one."

"Thanks."

I threw pitch after pitch. They flew straight into Allan's glove.

Afterward Asher and Bo both told me I had a good arm. Coach said, "Good practice."

I danced to the FourTrax. "You're the man," Nicky said, climbing on behind me. "You're the man."

I grinned. I couldn't wait to tell someone.

"Let's go throw some more," Nicky said. "You're on fire!"

"Naw. I've got something I have to do." I turned down the dirt road that led to Nicky's house, then stopped in his yard. "I'll call you later."

"Oh." Nicky hopped off and grabbed his gear. "Okay then."

"Hey, Nick," I called as he walked away. "Thanks for helping me."

"No big thing," Nicky said. He gave me a thumbs-up.

I started the FourTrax and headed back into town, whistling. Head pitcher.

I couldn't wait to tell Grandad.

26

I pulled up to the clinic and was surprised to see so many cars parked all over the lawn. Uncle Del and Aunt V, Mom and Dad, Pastor Harley, the Princesses, Charles the First, Greg, Gabby, Lou, and some people I didn't know were all in the room when I walked in.

Before I even looked at the bed, I knew something was really wrong. Mom's eyes were red and puffy. Dad's cap was pulled low over his eyes. Greg was slumped in the chair.

All around me people were sniffling and crying. For a minute I just listened to their soft sounds, and then I ran out of the room. I heard everyone calling, but I cranked the FourTrax and gunned it until I couldn't hear anything but the engine. Grandad was dead.

I rode the perimeter road of Kinnaman Ranch. The tires spat gravel as I went sliding around corners. "He's dead! He's dead!" I screamed it at the top of my lungs.

It felt like someone else was driving, someone else yelling and crying. I turned onto the logging road and geared down. I passed the ranger and four men but didn't stop. Higher and higher I climbed until I saw the salmonberry bush. I nosed the FourTrax between the ferns and rode until I could see the corner of the tree house, nestled up high.

I climbed up the ladder and shoved on the trapdoor. I stood at the rail. The sun was setting, turning the whole valley a deep gold.

Opening the toolbox, I grabbed the hammer and examined the floorboards until I found a nail head poked up, working its way out of the wood. I hammered it back in and beat on it a couple more times for good measure. Then I found another one. And another. *Bam! Bam! Bam!* The sound filled the air, drowning out everything else. When all the nail heads were pounded flat, I kept on, beating dents into the old wood. I beat the soft, worn railing and the walls and the floor until sweat dripped off my nose.

In the distance, I could hear men shouting and bushes crashing. Feet pounded and lantern lights bobbed between the trees. Three shots were fired, so loud that my ears rang. I didn't care. I lay on the floor, staring at the grain of the pine boards, tiny cracks and scratches and splinters no wider than a hair.

It wasn't true that Kinnaman Ranch was always growing and changing. Sometimes it shrank, got weaker, broke apart.

I climbed down, letting the trapdoor slam shut. I decided I didn't ever want to see this tree house again.

It was dark when I got home. I went straight to the barn.

I remembered Elmo's tongue hanging out from between his teeth, and his dull eyes. I sighed. I was ready to drag his body out to the pit and burn it on top of Snow's ashes if I had to. I would do the work in front of me.

I piled some wood into the fire pit. Then I held the flare from my kit to the kindling until the wood caught fire.

I didn't think my throat could squeeze any tighter, but it did, to where I could barely breathe by the time I turned and went to the tack room.

I put my hand on the doorknob and thought about praying. But what good would that do if it was already over? I shoved on the door, prepared for a cloud of buzzing flies and the horrible smell. I held my breath as the door creaked open.

I couldn't believe what I saw.

Elmo's head rose, his long neck swinging around toward me. His big shiny eyes blinked, and he hummed.

27

I ran to him. He raised his head to my hand and bumped it with his nose. Hungry.

His fever was gone, his eyes were bright and wet. And he was *humming*.

"Hey. Hey, boy." I knelt next to him. He sniffed at my lips, tickling me with his whiskers. "Hey." He snorted at my cheek. I wiped my eyes. "Are you hungry? You want a bottle?"

His whiskers tickled my neck and I laughed.

I grabbed the jar and ran to milk Bessie. Elmo gobbled it all down. If he'd been human, he would have burped. He looked at me as if to say, "Is that it?"

"I can't get any more just yet," I explained, petting his back. "Bessie's got to make more. She isn't a soda fountain, you know."

Elmo bumped my hand and nibbled the cuff of my shirt.

Then I noticed he was shivering. I covered him up with my sleeping bag, but I could still feel him shaking through the bag, scared little trembles.

"It's okay, buddy." I patted him. I got my wagon, put the sleeping bag in the bottom of it, then gently lifted Elmo in, careful not to bump his splint. I wheeled him outside, where the fire blazed in the burn pit. I parked him close so he could get warm.

I turned a log on its end and sat watching the flames dance and swirl and send sparks into the black night. Elmo curled his neck around to his shoulder and fell asleep, breathing deep and slow.

I threw one more log on the fire and when I got tired, I stretched out on the ground, using another log for a pillow.

Right before I fell asleep, I did pray, that God would give Grandad a message. Elmo was getting better. He was going to be okay. I would make sure of that.

"Hey, JT."

I felt Mom's hand on my shoulder and opened my eyes. It was still night, the full moon right above my head. The fire had burned down to a few red embers and the flare had burned out. I stood up. "Mom?"

Mom didn't say anything, just opened her arms.

I hugged her, burying my face in her flannel jacket.

After a while she said, "We were wondering where you'd gone."

"Just did some stuff."

"They caught the bear." She sat on a log. "Rogue boar."

"Yeah?" I checked Elmo. He was breathing fine. "Where at?"

"Little Sister. Near the second ridge."

"By the tree house?" Goose bumps rose on my arms.

"Yeah. Over that way." She looked at me. "Why?"

I shrugged, staring at the flames. I wondered how close the bear had come to the tree house. Sounded like it was pretty close. I glanced at the mountain, black against the night sky. I was safe up there, like always.

"You want to come inside and go to bed?"

I looked at Elmo, asleep in the wagon. "Can I bring him with me?"

"Ordinarily I'd say no."

"I know." I pulled the edge of the sleeping bag over Elmo's shoulder. "Never mind. I'd rather stay in the barn with him anyway."

"It's supposed to get colder tonight."

"I'm okay," I said.

She kicked the fire with her boot, spreading it out. Smoke drifted into the night air.

"Where's Dad?"

"Inside with Greg and Gabby."

"Oh."

"Funeral's Friday."

I threw a piece of wood into the embers.

"We picked out a casket. They're flying it from Anchorage tomorrow. It's mahogany. His favorite." She coughed.

"I'm going to need another sleeping bag." I stood up.

"JT, I know this is hard. Your granddad loved you very much."

I nodded. "Would you get the other sleeping bag for me?" I asked. "I don't feel like going in there."

She nodded, looking at me with a sad expression on her face.

I waited for Mom to bring the sleeping bag, then wheeled Elmo back to the tack room, milked Bessie, and fed Elmo another rubber glove of milk. He slurped it in about three seconds. His stitches were smooth and the skin was pale pink around them. His ears were soft and cool. I thought about going to my room—all that space that used to be Grandad's, empty now.

I petted Elmo for a while and then lay down next to him, sniffing his baby-llama straw smell. "We'll get along, boy," I said, just before I turned over and fell asleep.

28

Everyone in Fireweed put on clean hickory shirts and tying shoes and went to the cemetery. Pastor Harley said a few words. Then the men put Grandad's mahogany casket in the ground next to Grandma Rose's grave. We took turns throwing in a handful of dirt, and Pastor Harley said a long prayer. Every time we bowed our heads, the Kinnaman men wiped their eyes and their noses. The women bawled all the way through. So did Gabby. So did I.

When we were walking away from the grave, Lou put her arm around my shoulders and said, "How about you come on and have a piece of warm apple pie?"

When she said that, I started crying all over again. She hugged me to her soft side and said, "There now, baby. There now." She held me a long time, until Dad came over and picked me up. I put my face on his neck and got it all wet with my tears.

Dad carried me to Lou's and sat in a booth, but I still didn't look up as the Kinnamans and our friends ate and drank all around me. I remembered Grandad saying he looked forward to walking gold streets with Grandma Rose and sipping coffee at a place like Lou's. I cried more tears than I knew I had.

"Poor baby," said Lou to Dad. "Tough row to hoe, as close as they were and all."

"It has been a bad few weeks," Dad agreed. "Pop getting sick, and the bear. Joey's got a crippled cria at home to top it off."

I arched my back when I heard that and jumped off him. "He's not, either! He's better!"

The whole family was looking at me. I knew I was acting like a baby but I couldn't help it.

"Son," Dad said.

"Well, he keeps on getting better, and that's something." I crossed my arms. Dad didn't get it. On a ranch, some came and some went, but there was always hope.

29

When I walked in to feed Elmo that afternoon, he was standing on three legs, humming his wild music. He nibbled the edge of my jacket and took a wobbly step toward the water.

I knelt down and hugged him gently around his neck. He nibbled my ear, his fuzzy lips tickling me. He pulled and pulled at the glove, finishing his milk in record time. He bumped me again, wanting more. Then I had an idea. If he could stand, he could nurse. "Just a minute, buddy," I said, then ran to the kitchen for the vanilla bottle. Vanilla was the only scent strong enough to cover up a llama's natural scent, making it perfect for adoptions. A little vanilla on the cria, a little more on the dam, and they think they know each other. It was a trick Grandad had taught me.

I put Elmo in my wagon, gently lifting his splinted leg to hang over the edge. I wheeled him out of the tack room, down the aisle to Bessie's stall. Then I poured vanilla in my hand and rubbed the brown liquid on Bessie's nose. She snorted and sneezed. I rubbed vanilla on Elmo's nose, and on his neck and back. Then I lifted him up, stepped inside the stall, and set him down on the yellow straw. I stood back to watch.

Elmo sniffed the straw and bawled. Bessie stepped toward him, sniffing him gently at first. She sniffed his head, his ears, his nose, his legs. Then she whiffled his nose and he whiffled her, humming.

When she stepped closer, Elmo bumped her belly, nuzzling for the milk. I held my breath. She raised her back leg. Bessie would either let him suckle or kick him away. Her hoof flexed.

Then she burped up some cud and started humming, setting her hoof on the straw. Elmo sucked noisily, wagging his tail.

It had worked.

Later, I went hiking on Little Sister Mountain. I hiked over the first ridge and up the second. The late-afternoon sun made long shadows and slices of gold air between the trees. Before long, I saw the salmonberry bush and Grandad's trail, and my feet turned and followed it to the base of the tree house. I climbed the ladder, looking at our initials in the tree trunk, remembering the day Grandad had carved mine into the bark along with everyone else's.

Sitting on the floor, looking out over the ranch and the valley, I squeezed my eyes shut tight. I saw Grandad sitting across from me, betting pretzels on his poker hand and laughing. I saw him next to me, leaning over the rail, pointing toward the inlet, toward Denali, toward the stars. I saw him following Old Timer's path as the eagle flew across the valley. I could almost feel Grandad's gnarled hand on mine, his pale blue eyes smiling out at the world.

But when I opened my eyes, I was alone. I looked out the window. Big Sister sloped toward the valley. Our ranch lay nestled between the mountains, the creeks drawing a crooked line around our land. Kinnaman Ranch. Grandad's footsteps were all over this valley. His footprints were probably still in the half-frozen mud by the fence. They were here, on the worn floorboards he'd built. And then I got it—I knew why his tree house was someplace special to hold on to.

30

As spring wore into summer, Elmo kept on growing. I left him alone for a while, letting him get to know Bessie and heal on his own. It wasn't long before he got around pretty well with three steps and a hop.

The day he started putting weight on his leg, I decided to try an idea I had to help his weak leg muscles get stronger. I took the piece of canvas from my kit and folded it into a long wide rectangle: a sling.

I cut the bandages and took off Elmo's splint. His leg looked small, with the black fiber all matted down. I looped the canvas under his stomach, near his back legs.

"Stand," I told him. It was like he knew I was trying to help him. He obediently stood, holding his back hoof off the ground. I gripped the sling and lifted along with him, supporting his hurt leg. He took just a few steps, then sat down. I gave him a biscuit and told him, "Good llama."

My idea was to help him get stronger, little by little. At first he didn't like it, but each day he took a few more steps on his healing leg, until he could walk up and down the aisle.

Then one morning he walked to the end of the aisle and wouldn't budge from the closed barn door. He craned his neck, sniffing and snuffling at the warm air. It was time to take him outside. I was nervous about leading him but I knew I couldn't leave Elmo in the barn all his life. We walked to the corral, me following just behind, hunched over his rump, holding the sling above his hips and supporting his leg, and he acted like he didn't even know I was there. He investigated everything—the slats, the latch, the dirt, and the old dung on the ground. We made a wide circle in the corral. Step, step, step, support. Around we went in a wide circle.

When I thought he'd had enough exercise for the day, I told him to stop near the gate.

"Cush," I said. I gently let the sling go as he settled himself to the ground. He bumped my knee with his nose and I gave him a biscuit, scratching his neck. "Good llama," I said.

"What are your plans for him?" Greg came in and knelt beside us.

"Get him healed up first," I said, blushing. "Maybe train him to pull a cart someday."

Greg nodded. "That sling is a pretty good idea."

That was a Kinnaman Ranch compliment. "Thanks," I said. I'd been afraid Greg would think it was stupid.

"You know, I'm taking Tumtum over to the back field today," said Greg. "Getting ready for breeding season. You could come with me if you want."

"I don't want to go anywhere near that mule," I said, and spat.

Greg laughed. "Some llamas are just harder to get along with. Tumtum's one of them. But he's not so terrible. You'll see. All it takes is time."

I hoped so. Some days it seemed like all I had was time now that Grandad was gone. Still, it felt good to know Greg believed in me.

Elmo got stronger and stronger, and before long, he was running and playing with the other crias in the midnight sun. I started loading him with my survival kit and backpack, and he never once sat down. He followed me like a pup and when we went fishing at Bobcat Creek, he lay at my feet. His limp was so small you'd really have to look to notice it.

The Eagles went to the championship, and it's a

simple fact that I helped some. I didn't pitch a no-hitter, but I struck out a few and I knew there was always next year. When we won, Coach gave me the huge trophy and told me I'd earned it. I took it home and put it on Grandad's side of the room. It made a nice place to hang my cap.

Greg built a cria-size cart for Elmo to pull. He used some pieces from my strike box. That was okay by me, because it was time for that wood to be made into something else. Next year I would need a new one anyway. I was getting taller and Grandad said the strike zone would change as I grew.

As soon as the rented packers returned from hiking the wilderness of Alaska, it would be shearing season on Kinnaman Ranch. Uncle Del and Aunt V promised to come for two weeks and help shear, card the fiber, wash it, and spin it into yarn. Then the buyers would come. We'd sell fiber, guards, what was left of the bachelor herd, and some packers. There was still hope for Kinnaman Ranch.

One night in late summer, Dad was playing the piano and Mom was knitting a slipper. Greg and I were finishing a game of checkers at the table.

"I think our youngest is becoming quite a llama farmer," Mom said, her needles clicking. "I've seen him cush Elmo with just hand signals. Grandad would be proud."

My heart twinged for just a second. But then I was

okay. He *would* be proud, and that made me feel good. I moved my checker. "King me."

Dad looked up from the piano keys and said, "Then it's time you bring in the herds."

I looked up. "Me?" I glanced at Greg.

"You're winning anyway," Greg said. "Go on."

My stomach curled with relief and a little bit of fear, but I stood and said "Yes, sir." I started toward the machine shed for the FourTrax, but it was such a clear, still night, the sky all orangey red, I wanted to walk.

I filled my pockets with biscuits and walked along the perimeter road. Another quiet evening in a string of quiet summer evenings. Even great ball games seemed like quiet victories. I missed Grandad's voice calling out, "Attaboy!"

I wished he could see me now. I wished I could talk to him.

I decided to start with Sentry's third-year guards. I'd know right away if I could handle the rest of the herds or if I still needed help. In the field, Sentry's neck went straight up as I approached the herd. Then they all looked up, ears perked forward. Sentry stepped toward me, sniffing. I held out my hand and he whiffled it.

The llamas Grandad loved so much gathered all around me, sniffing at my pockets and humming. Their velvety noses tickled my hands and tugged at my cap. If I still had his llamas, if I could still do what he loved to do in the place he'd called home, didn't I still have a little bit of him? I took a breath. *"Come, llamas,"* I called softly into the gathering dark. I expected Sentry to ignore my command, like usual. *"Come, llamas."* As I said the words I'd heard Grandad say so many times, I could almost hear him. I called over and over, "Come, llamas, come on."

From high up on the mountain, Old Timer took flight. He climbed quickly, his white head glinting in the sun and his keen eyes on the fields below. He tipped his wings and soared across the valley. I felt like the Denali wood frog thawing out after a hard winter.

Maybe Kinnaman Ranch was always growing and changing, but in different ways. Sometimes it was plain numbers, like when crias were born or guards were sold. But sometimes it was invisible, like learning to see where the hope was, or doing things you couldn't do before. All you could really do was keep on keeping on, just like Grandad said.

I took a deep breath and tried again. "Come, llamas. Come on."

Sentry swung his head around, signaling the herd in the unspoken llama way. I turned and began walking. I didn't have to glance back. I heard the soft padded steps over the grass. They were following me.

About the Author

Jennifer Morris grew up in Oregon and earned an MFA in creative writing from the University of Alaska. She lives in Mississippi with her husband and their three children. *Come, Llamas* is her first novel.